Jack Waters

BY

Scott Adlerberg

BROKEN RIVER BOOKS
EL PASO, TX

for Chaits

THE FIRST DEBT

Around the turn of the nineteenth century, near the City of New Orleans, there lived a man named Jack Waters. Throughout Louisiana, among gamblers, he had a reputation. His specialty was poker. He liked draw poker and five card stud, and his skill was such that he won more often than he lost. Jack Waters loved the challenge and excitement of gambling, but his deep blue eyes always held a look of slight dissatisfaction. He believed that a man, a gentleman anyhow, should gamble for the sheer fun of it, while he, on the contrary, did it to support himself.

Waters came from a slave-owning family that had lost all its wealth in the Civil War. From his father, who was killed at the Battle of Shiloh when he was one, he had inherited a mansion outside the city.

Here he lived, the last of his line, preferring to a wife the company of whores in the French Quarter. He retained a Creole cook and a black maid. Over the old estate where cotton had grown before Sherman's men burned it, he would ride his jet-black colt through the weeds and cypresses. Waters was a crack shot with a rifle and from time to time would enter the bayou to hunt birds and alligators. Though rugged as a Cajun, he looked urbane, with his short brown hair, smooth jaw line, and pencil sharp nose. He had a charming smile and his manners were polished. Even to his gambling friends, he was a generous host. The maid would fix the guest rooms, and for days on end, while he and others played cards, the chef would serve gumbo, oysters, and jambalaya. Sometimes he wished he had lived before the war, when slaves would have done all his work for him, but if he was not a true man of leisure, at least gambling allowed him to avoid real labor.

Now apart from his skills, benefitting them, Waters kept a cool head. No one had ever seen him get angry at the poker table. Up or down, winning or losing, he showed his opponents a suave exterior. He would declare his bets in a toneless voice, "I call," or "I raise," and he would push his chips forward without so much as a flicker of an eyelash. If at the end of a night he'd won, he would smile faintly but without a trace of pride or gloating. If he had lost, he would rise from the table, yawn nonchalantly, and congratulate the winners. Other gamblers envied his consistent success, but they admired his self-control.

Only two things could ruffle his poise. One involved the keeping of accounts. Waters rarely borrowed money, but when he did, he repaid his lender promptly. His credit rating among other gamblers was high, and he never welshed on a debt. The problems came when people took advantage of him. Those who were slow to pay *their* debts would be transfixed by an unnerving sight. Waters' tan skin would turn red, his eyes would get narrow, and the veins in his brow would bulge.

"If you're a gambler, you must be straight in your dealings with money. This is our first rule of conduct."

One man, a visitor from Kansas City, laughed when Waters said this, and he hooted with outright glee when Waters, insulted by his show of mirth, asked for satisfaction.

"What world are you living in?" the other replied. "You'll get your money when I have it to give."

But maybe Waters thought he was holding the cash. Because the next night, in the French Quarter, in a dark alleyway near his hotel, the man was found with his throat cut. Policemen checked his pockets and examined his room, but they never came across his wallet. Though nobody could prove anything, the rumor spread that Waters had killed him.

Years later, another incident occurred. A man in a game Waters was playing in tried to cheat. This was a mistake. Waters had less tolerance for card sharps than he did for welshers. Just talking about such people made fire appear in his eyes and speckles of froth pop out on his lips. Maybe cheating players had fleeced him in the past, but he doubted it. He knew all the tricks and every time he played poker he watched for irregular moves and glances. On this occasion, the culprit was a baby-faced twenty-two year old, the son of a wealthy New Orleans businessman. He had been playing cards throughout Louisiana, and sources had it that some on the riverboats were labeling him a prodigy. Undaunted by the praise for the newcomer, keen to take him on, Waters invited him to his house for an overnight game with the best veterans. But perhaps the kid got worried on his end, anxious to ensure that he would beat them. Waters caught him rigging a shuffle, and his face swelled up with blood.

"In my house!" he roared. "I invite him as a guest and he cheats!"

The veterans, shocked by this outburst, beseeched him to restrain himself. Waters kept shouting, however, and under this onslaught, the youngster twitched. As if to make amends for his act, he threw all his money on the table, but the motion brought cards sliding out of his shirt sleeves.

"I'm sorry, I'm sorry," he kept wailing, and he rose to leave.

His craven behavior made Waters even angrier. The boy had the gall to cheat in his house, and then to think he could depart unscathed. In a flash, like a panther, Waters leapt over the round oak table, scattering cards and chips. He jumped onto the boy and they fell to the floor. The others yanked at his arms and shoulders, but they couldn't get a grip on him. Waters pushed them away. He drew from under his shirt the long retractable knife he always carried for protection, and ignoring the boy's cries for mercy, stabbed him in the heart.

This time he'd gone too far. There were four witnesses, and the victim was the son of an influential man. The veterans sympathized with him, since they too hated cheaters, but once he had calmed down a bit, they told him he should flee. None of them, old acquaintances all, wanted to turn him in, but sooner or later they would have to tell the sheriff about the killing. They urged him to leave the state or, better yet, the country.

Waters wasted no time. Already he had regained his composure. He took all the money in the bedroom safe, eighty-six thousand dollars, and gave five thousand to one of the men.

"Give half to my cook, half to the maid. For their years of faithful service."

The remaining cash, balled up in his clothes, he put in a leather rucksack, and he saddled the fastest horse on his estate. The night was dark. A wind purred in the cypresses. Waters knew he had acted rashly, that he had let his temper overwhelm him, but his only regret was for the inconvenience he'd brought upon himself, ruining his comfortable life.

Near Lake Pontchartrain, he dismounted, bidding his colt farewell. Then, carrying the rucksack over one shoulder, he walked to St. Philip Street and knocked on the door of a private residence. A window above him opened, and a man stepped onto the balcony.

Waters greeted him. He was a hunting companion, a white-haired Frenchman in retirement after a career as a mercenary soldier. All over the world, fighting in wars, he had found lucrative employment, and upstairs in the lamplit study Waters explained the situation. Then he asked a favor. He wondered whether his friend could use his foreign and maritime contacts to help him get settled in another country. It had to be a country where poker was popular because he had no intention of working for his money.

The Frenchman suggested Monaco, but Waters said he would like a rough land. When not gambling, he would want to hunt and ride horses, and he would love to have a forest nearby, to remind him of Louisiana's bayous.

"You're asking for a lot," the Frenchman said, but he knew of a place.

As a mercenary, he had once fought on a Caribbean island. In this former Spanish colony, now calling itself a republic, he'd helped the army crush a peasant revolt. He'd given advice to General Hernandez Garcia Napoles, the country's president. Gambling was legal in the capital there, and you could arrange poker games in the casinos. In fact, the President himself liked to play cards. The island had forests where you could hunt and hills where you could go riding, but Waters would have to learn Spanish. He said he could do that, and the Frenchman said "good." As a side light, though, he told Waters not to get involved in politics. Power struggles and rebellions were common and proclaiming loyalty to any group could be unwise. If he made it clear to anyone who asked him that he had no interest in the nation's internal affairs, he would probably be safe, no matter who was in the government. Waters said he could do that also, as he despised politics.

The Frenchman was satisfied, and for the next fortnight, while Waters hid in his apartment, he worked to find him a passage on a banana boat returning to the island. One captain was taking a ship there, and with a bundle of Waters' money, the Frenchman persuaded the man to transport the fugitive. On the day Waters was to leave, his friend wrote him several letters of introduction to people he knew lived on the island. Included was a letter to the General himself.

But the Frenchman also gave him a warning: "Don't play cards with Hernandez Garcia. He hates to lose, especially to gringos."

* * *

For two and a half months Jack Waters played no poker; he merely acquainted himself with his new surroundings. He studied Spanish from grammar books and he practiced his diction with the people his friend had told him to call on. Most of them were rich landowners of Spanish descent, or they were government officials connected to General Garcia. Waters impressed them with how quickly he was learning their language, and the elegance of his deportment, they remarked among themselves, was unusual for a gringo. He never revealed why he'd come to their island, but he entertained them with his risqué tales about the French quarter. Waters had plenty of amusing gambling stories to tell and he proved himself a stout drinker — he could hold his rum. Soon he had ingratiated himself into the republic's upper social circles, and he saw that their members, an aristocracy, led the same sort of leisurely existence he had led in New Orleans.

There was much about this place that he welcomed. The weather was hot and humid. The capital was a port city. Like the French Quarter, it had a European look, with outdoor cafés and grillwork balconies. The Spanish-colonial churches were layered with white stucco, and palm trees and statues decorated the plazas. Life was slow, as it was at home; people took siestas every afternoon and in the early evenings would stop to have a chat with friends in the square.

Waters took a room in a two-floor hotel that contained a courtyard. In this enclosure was a garden, and from the tiled patio outside his door he could smell the carnations and hibiscus; he could watch green hummingbirds flitting between the pink and purple flowers. A man down the street owned a stable, and Waters would pay him to borrow a horse. With it he explored the country. Outside the capital, the republic's only city, were villages, farms, highlands, and bush. Waters bought a rifle for hunting and a machete which he taught himself how to use. Once or twice, in the forest, bandits with pistols robbed him, and he always attracted wary stares when he rode by the thatch-roofed, bamboo huts that composed most village dwellings. To be the focus of this attention made him smile, and as he had in the bayou, where the vigilant Cajuns lived, he tried to be civil and to speak with the locals. He would drink cheap rum in the cantinas and he frequented the crumbling wooden shacks where the rural prostitutes had their beds. In haunts like these, he spoke with men quite different from the ones he knew in the city, men who were poor and who hated the very landowners he found pleasant and hospitable. Among them were Latinos and blacks who worked all day on the sugar plantations. They wore straw hats and filthy rags and went home to their wives and children every night to eat red beans with rice. Chickens in their yards provided eggs; if lucky, they ate a meal with beef, pork or goat once a week. They reminded him of the white sharecroppers and the blacks back home, though here on the island, field workers had soldiers for company. Ever since the last uprising four years earlier, troops with rifles had been patrolling the larger haciendas. These sentinels belonged to the republic's army, a mixture of foreign professionals and surly recruits who wore dull green uniforms. The sight of them always irritated Waters. They looked threatening, and he imagined that Yankee soldiers living off Confederate farmland during the Civil War had looked similar.

One evening, in his hotel room, he mentioned these impressions he had to a couple of his landowning acquaintances. They were all sitting at a table, having drinks. The older of his guests, a potbellied graybeard, laughed at his words, but said it was not a wise idea for him to take pity on the nation's laborers.

"You shouldn't mix with those illiterates anyway," he continued. "It's bad for your Spanish, the grammar they use."

Waters grinned, but the second man, who wore a silk shirt from Paris and alligator shoes from North America, began to yell at him. Like the first man, he owed his wealth to sugar plantations passed on by his father, but unlike his friend he seemed to have taken Waters' comments personally.

"Don't you come from New Orleans? Didn't your relatives own slaves? Who are you to question our methods? We aren't stupid, señor. We know how you Southerners treat your Negroes. Worse than we Spanish have treated ours."

Waters' face turned a light shade of red. Tempted to rise, he crossed his ankles and took a sip of his hot buttered rum. Only then did his normal skin color return, and he displayed a blank poker countenance.

"I happen to be descended from slave owners," he said, closing one eye. "But I don't have nothin' against wealthy Negroes. I'd as soon play cards with five rich niggers as I would with five rich whites. The color of the money's no different."

He meant this statement as a joke, but he failed to lighten the mood of the gathering. His guests scowled and glared at him. They finished their drinks and said good night. And now, despite the letters of introduction he had been given by the mercenary, the reputable Frenchman, many of the island's rich inhabitants grew suspicious of Jack Waters.

They held meetings to discuss and analyze him, dissecting everything he'd said about their country. Since nobody knew why he had come to live in the republic, his excursions into the hills and forest suddenly seemed mysterious. Here, affluent people stayed in the capital, as the bankers and the President's ministers did, or, like the big landowners and retired generals, they spent their time on their haciendas. They didn't explore the bush and highlands; when traveling through the wild, they stuck to the dirt roads. For in those wild sections were the bandits, the peons in their villages, the incendiaries who'd escaped death in the previous rebellion and were still trying to foment revolution. The aristocrats trusted the army to deal with them; there were barracks and command posts dotting the countryside. But from the peculiar way he was shuttling between the two worlds, mingling freely with both the peasants and the social elite, it was obvious that Waters might be a spy. He might be giving the rebels information about the landed class. Even worse, he might be a gunrunner arranging shipments of ammunition from exiles and subversives in his own country. This was 1904, and the wildfire of anarchism was raging across the globe. Just three years ago, one of those apostles of random violence had shot and killed the President of the United States. Maybe he belonged to that lunatic fraternity. These were the things the landowners were saying about Jack Waters, and whatever they said reached the ears of the alert army colonels, who in turn reported the gossip and speculation to their boss, the President, General Hernandez Garcia Napoles.

Waters, for his part, was unaware of this talk. The rumor mongers hid their sentiments by speaking in whispers or behind his back. Yet they did not sever their ties to him, the better to keep an eye on him, and would frequently ask that he play cards at their new haciendas. Other times he played in the hotel casinos. He would sit at the shiny, mahogany tables in the carpeted rooms tucked away from the noise of rolling dice, the spinning roulette wheels, the croupiers. There would be people from throughout the Americas, and night after night he would find himself sitting with an assortment of visitors: Cubans who owned cigar factories, Haitians who owned sugar estates, South American generals, colonial entrepreneurs of the British, French, and Dutch West Indies. He had lost none of his sharpness. In three weeks he doubled his original bankroll. He was really enjoying his life here, and using an assumed name, he wrote to the Frenchman and told him so. "You picked the right place for me to go. I get on well with people, and I've been apolitical, as we said I should. No one could possibly think I have the least interest in their country's affairs. I speak about other subjects and try never to affront. I avoid all potential intrigues."

He was not naive, however. He knew that the island might be swept up by a storm. Another eruption of violence was supposed to be imminent, and he could feel the tension around him. Every day the republic's newspaper said something about the rebels in the countryside. They were massing their forces to attack the capital and would try to assassinate General Garcia. They would set fire to plantations, like they had four years ago, and would slaughter any peasants who put up resistance to joining them. The paper supported the government, so its reports were often exaggerated, but in truth, the landowners did have reason to be nervous. Dreadful events plagued their haciendas, despite the presence of the watchful soldiers. Pigs, cows, and horses would die in their stalls, black-lipped and bloated, the victims of poisonings. House servants could no longer could be trusted; in the cribs of the oligarchs' babies, gray rats were sometimes found, gnawing at an infant's fingers and toes. Men were paid to spy and report on their peon companions, and the ones spied on, whenever they uncovered these informers, not only killed them, but as a warning to others, cut off their heads and impaled them on the tops of sugar cane stalks.

Rebels were everywhere. The man who did his work without complaint by day might be a man who plotted revolution in his village after dark. And of all the snakes hiding in the republic's grass, one in particular commanded the respect of the discontented. His name was Raoul Cardenes Amoros, and if the President considered any single person the leader of the incendiary movement, it was he. Amoros lived somewhere in the forested highlands. For seventeen years, through five unsuccessful revolts and three consecutive military governments, he and his band of volunteer sharpshooters, The Fifty, had carried on their war. They robbed banks in the capital, they kidnapped wealthy citizens and demanded huge ransoms, they engineered periodic raids on the military stations throughout the country. General Garcia always denounced them as "ruthless bandits, nothing more. The money they take from their murders and robberies goes into their pockets, nowhere else." Yet few peasants believed the President when he made his accusations; instead, among themselves, they spoke about the thousands of acres of fertile farmland that he, Hernandez Garcia, possessed. They referred to the deal supposedly signed with the casino owners, all of whom were foreigners, men from Europe or the States, an agreement that allowed them to run their casinos without restrictions so long as they gave him a quarter of their profits every day. To the poor and the landless, Amoros was a legend, a Robin Hood figure. "He steals from the rich to turn gold into guns." This was the saying prevalent among them.

As it so happened, Jack Waters had met this man. About two months after his arrival on the island, he and the rebel had conversed. This had occurred during a trip he took into the forest, when, early in the evening, in a small village, he had tied up his horse and entered a cantina. The bar was a hut with wooden walls and a flat tin roof. An oil lamp surrounded by moths and flies dangled from a hooked nail in the ceiling. Behind the counter was a wall stocked with bottles of rum and the local fruit wines, and men dirty and sweaty, who had worked all day in the fields, lolled against the counter or sat at the circular tables near it. The place was noisy, filled with the sounds of humorous cursing and raucous laughter. The stench of cigar smoke hung in the air. Waters, seated at a table, was telling someone about a prostitute he'd had the other night, and as he spoke, he and the man kept sipping from their glasses of rum. Then a third man pulled up a chair and joined them. Extending his right hand, he introduced himself. Waters shook it with a firm grip. Though he said nothing, he remembered Amoros from newspaper pictures and posters inside the capital's Post Office. His nose was flat and his lips were wide, like an African's, but his long black hair was as straight as any Spaniard's. He had an almond-nut complexion and cold black eyes and in the black shirt he was wearing, he had a vaguely sinister appearance, enhanced by his cadaverous thinness. He looked, with his gravity, like a leader, and waving one arm at the table, he dismissed the other man who was there. The man withdrew. Amoros stared at Waters, scrutinizing him, and getting no response from the poker player, leaned forward and spoke. He addressed Waters in Castilian Spanish, a Spanish that had been learned in schools. From his utter directness, Waters doubted their meeting was a coincidence, and when he broke his silence to say this, Amoros confirmed it. Sometime ago, he said, men who belonged to his group The Fifty had called his attention to the gringo at large. Curious about the stranger, he'd told them to watch Jack Waters when he hunted and when he socialized in the village bars. And they had done this, observing him for a solid month, returning to say that the gringo was an able horseman and an excellent shot. He also, oddly enough, appeared to mix well with the common people, even the blacks. Amoros had been more intrigued than ever to hear this and had decided then to meet the Yankee.

"I'm no Yankee," Waters said. "I come from New Orleans."

Amoros asked him why he'd left there. As always, Waters said he had moved for a change of scenery. Amoros conceded that his country had splendid scenery, but then he declared with anger in his voice that as long as generals and landowners ruled it, the island would look stained to him. He gave examples of injustices that the oligarchs, through the years, had committed, and he did not seem to notice anything when Waters yawned, impatient to leave. Waters shifted in his chair, and at last Amoros came out and said why he had been seeking the interview — would Waters like to join The Fifty? Amoros was convinced he was a man of the people, and with his shooting and riding abilities, he could make a terrific fighter.

"We need every man we can find to help us overthrow the regime."

Waters thanked him for the offer, which he took as a compliment, but said he could not yoke himself to the rebels. He explained his policy of political neutrality. He said he was not afraid to fight for a cause, as his father and uncles had done in the Civil War, but to be honest he had never found one that stirred his emotions. Injustice was present here, but it was also everywhere else in the world. *C'est la vie.*

The revolutionary shook his head, disappointed. He tried to get Waters to reconsider but Waters said that becoming a mountain fighter would mean giving up poker. He'd have to do that because he never played cards with poor people. He could not take their hardearned money, for one thing, and it bored him to play for low stakes.

"Do you have to gamble?" Amoros asked.

"I do to make money," Waters said. "And to keep my comforts. The bush is a nice place to visit, not to live."

On this note, they parted. Waters didn't know if the rebel leader had told his supporters anything about their discussion, but the peasants remained cordial to him regardless. For this hospitality, he was secretly grateful. He would not have wanted to end his horseback trips, nor to confine himself to the city and the haciendas of his wealthy acquaintances. He had no way of knowing that this tight-knit flock, though they knew nothing of his meeting with Amoros, still regarded him with mistrust. They kept telling General Garcia that he must be a rebel agent. How else could they interpret his visits to the forest? People had advised him to stop doing that, saying it was hazardous for his health, but he continued his excursions while maintaining their salutary effect. By now, they presumed that he gave their enemies a major part of his winnings, and they acknowledged to the President that he was a poker wizard. Time after time when they played with him, he would beat them all.

Eventually the day came when the General got tired of hearing about this gringo. Like his enemy

Amoros, he'd become eager to meet Waters and form his own opinion about him, and one Monday morning, he mailed Waters a letter inviting him to the presidential palace that Saturday evening. Dinner would be served there, and afterward, with the other guests, a friendly game of poker would be played.

Waters recalled the Frenchman's warning: "Don't play cards with Hernandez Garcia. He hates to lose, especially to gringos." And he had his apprehensions about the wording of the President's letter; as he saw it, you could not have a "friendly" game of poker. Either you played seriously, with concentration, or you did not play at all. He thought about declining the invitation but feared that this would offend Garcia and create difficulties. What to do? He felt trapped, and in the end he sent a note saying he would come. He purchased a tuxedo for the occasion, but all week he wondered, for the first time in his life, whether he should lose intentionally. By making subtle errors, he could allow the General to beat him and to indulge in braggadocio.

The night of the dinner arrived. Waters found himself sitting in the marble-floored room where the Spanish governors had once held masquerades. Gilded chandeliers shone there, and gleaming white china and red lace covered the table. Besides Waters, there were three guests: a bearded army colonel, a young captain, and a landowner he knew. The latter also wore a tuxedo, but the military men, including the President, had on black boots and green uniforms. Garcia sat down at the head of the table, and Waters was given the chair immediately to his left. The General was a stubby-armed man with a protruding belly and a gray handlebar mustache. His skin was pale for the tropics, as though, ruling the country from the palace, he never saw the light of day. He perspired in torrents and had to keep using his napkin to wipe the rolls of rumpled flesh that were his cheeks.

Throughout the meal, he directed the course of conversation. As waiters in white jackets came and went, he kept asking Waters questions. He wanted to know if Waters had owned property in Louisiana, and when Waters described his estate and the way he had left it uncultivated, the General asked him why he hadn't rented his land to sharecroppers. Did he dislike having people work for him? No, Waters said, he did not, but his poker winnings had allowed him to live sumptuously without having to concern himself with the business of running a plantation.

"I see," said the General, and he asked Waters about his old social habits, about the type of people he had as his friends.

"All types," Waters said. "Why are you curious?"

Garcia simply frowned. He asked Waters whether he'd spent lots of time in the bayou, as he claimed, or if he had not, for certain reasons, started his jaunts into the forest after he came to the island.

"Certain reasons? What do you mean?"

The questions puzzled Waters, and he sensed that his answers, though truthfully given, were disturbing Garcia, who kept exchanging glances with the others.

After dinner, the President ordered the table to be cleared. He called for a deck of cards and a rack of chips. These were brought, and Waters, uneasy, took off his jacket and rolled up his sleeves to prepare for a game he had no desire to join. The men played all night. They smoked Havana cigars and dropped the ends onto the floor and every hour a servant would come in, supplying a decanter of aged rum. Garcia played with enthusiasm, but he was reckless. When dealt a mediocre hand, he would curse; when he received a good down card, the General could barely keep from smiling. The landowner and the military officers made the requisite miscalculations to let him win large pots, but Waters had something in his disposition that hated to see such poker incompetence go unpunished. He felt like an ass losing intentionally and could not bring himself to keep doing it. He stopped drinking. And as chance would have it, he drew exceptional cards for the night. The General was loath to fold his own cards — he always seemed to think that by some miracle he would pull a winning hand — and because of this blind trust in his luck, he lost more money than he should have.

They were between games, during a respite, when the General asked Waters another question.

"What do you do with the cash you win?"

"Save it for the next game."

"Or give it to your friends?" the General said.

"What friends?"

"You know. We all know who your friends are."

Waters looked at him closely, but gave the remark little thought. He needed to concentrate on his playing and assumed that the General was trying to distract him. Though he understood Garcia's frustration, he had no sympathy for him. After all, it was the General himself who had insisted on the game. By the time the five men decided to quit, which was at dawn, Garcia owed Waters 34,600 pesos, the equivalent of 29,800 dollars. As a sign of his gentlemanly nature and to show that he wanted no hard feelings to result, Waters extended his hand to the General. But the General did not shake it.

"Do you expect me to pay you?"

"How can you not? You owe me the money."

"I'm not giving you cash so you can enrich my enemies."

"I don't know what you mean," Waters said.

"The colonel here could take you to jail right now for your activities, but we don't like to arrest gringos. It causes headaches with your ambassador."

"Give him a week to leave the island," the colonel said.

Waters stared at the four men. They all sat motionless with their hands on the table, and they looked like members of a tribunal that had passed judgment on a prisoner.

"This is an outrage, General! You'd deport me because I beat you in a poker game?"

"One week to leave the capital. But if you enter the forest one more time we'll consider you fair game."

"That's it," the colonel said. "We warned you."

Waters squinted at Garcia, and the veins in his forehead swelled. His skin burned and prickled. Without even thinking he snatched at the knife under his shirt, but before he could touch it, the captain and the colonel jumped up from their seats, pointing revolvers at him.

"You'd better go," the President said. "Be off the island by next Saturday."

Waters tried to object again, but he was too choked with rage to speak another word. He stumbled away from the table, and the young captain escorted him from the palace. The morning air felt warm and sticky. Throughout the city, cocks were crowing, and though he heard these squawks every day and never experienced the least annoyance, he found them extremely grating now and pictured the birds laughing at him. They were ridiculing him with their hideous calls. He darted up the street, horrified, and continued to run till he reached his hotel room. There, out of breath, he sat at his table and poured himself a tall glass of rum. The alcohol helped to calm him, and he was able to think lucidly again.

At first he berated himself for having ignored the Frenchman's warning about the General. The intelligent thing would have been to decline Garcia's invitation, even if it meant offending the despicable man, or to have let him end the night a winner, top dog. Without a doubt he had been a fool, and to punish himself, to give himself a dose of pain, Waters ground his left hand into the sharp edge of the table. But then he stopped this self-chastisement, and his thoughts swung in a different direction. Back at the palace he'd been polite; his manners and decorum had been exemplary. He had played by the rules they picked for the games, as he always did when in someone else's house, and he had been ready to surrender his cash if he lost. Waters concluded that at the palace he had done nothing blameworthy.

The weekend passed and then two more days. Waters marched up and down the streets of the capital, silently brooding, wondering how to get the money that was rightly his. Once he stopped at the American Embassy, a regal white mansion near the port, but he backed off on going inside. He had left the United States as a murderer and a fugitive from justice. If he managed to see the ambassador, to whom he could lodge a formal complaint against Garcia, the diplomat might want to investigate his past before doing anything to help him collect his 34,600 pesos.

Waters started to ponder ways he could get near the President again. He would have liked to corner him alone, to threaten him with violence, but the fleshy stunted man was protected. An iron fence topped with spikes encircled the palace grounds, and armed soldiers were always stationed within and outside this barrier. To make matters worse, Garcia, ever fearful of rebel assassination attempts, rarely ventured beyond these confines. Waters abandoned the hope of intimidating him and resolved to turn to his acquaintances for counsel. Again and again he knocked on their doors. But the people who had been showering him with hospitality, wining and dining him in their homes, refused to see him. Each time he announced himself to the butler of an establishment, the man would say, "No, Mr. Waters. You can't come in." Waters would yell then, roaring into the entrance hall, entreating the master of the house to use his influence with Garcia and urge the man to pay his debt. But the servant would hastily close the door. Even when Waters relinquished his pride and did all but kneel to beg for help, the portal would be slammed shut. He could not believe it. The General had organized a conspiracy against him. A judge he approached in the city's municipal court laughed when he said that he wanted to file a lawsuit against Garcia and none of the lawyers he appealed to when he visited their offices would take his case for any price. Was there no higher legal authority here than General Garcia? Was there no one here who could redress this injustice?

On Wednesday, in his growing indignation, he came up with a new tack. He walked into the dingy office of the island's newspaper and offered to pay a substantial amount if the publisher would come to his assistance. On the front page of the next day's edition, the following words, in bold letters, were to be printed.

General Hernandez Garcia Napoles owes Señor Waters, a foreigner in this land, 34, 600 pesos. He lost the money in a poker game, but he refuses to honor the debt. This is a shameful act which I'm sure the gracious people of this beautiful country find appalling.

Under this long headline was to be an article detailing what had happened. Waters would write the story himself, and he hoped to embarrass Garcia so badly the contemptible man would have to pay him.

Now the publisher, who was bent-backed and elderly, had heard all about the poker game from the colonel who participated in it, and he knew the reason that the President stood fast in his refusal to give up a penny. He too was sure that Waters would deliver the money to rebel fighters, to Raoul Amoros himself perhaps. And yet, despite this conviction, he said he might publish the story.

"Name a fair price," Waters said.

"Thirty-four thousand six hundred pesos."

"Are you trying to be humorous?"

"Not at all. Anything less isn't worth the risk."

"Fair enough. I can get it back in the casinos."

The publisher asked for the money, but Waters said he would bring it tomorrow, after the paper, with his article prominent, was in nationwide circulation.

"You might take the money and do nothing. You might call the General and tell him to put soldiers after me."

"How do I know you'll pay me?" the publisher asked.

"Because I'm Jack Waters. My word is my bond."

The publisher scratched the bridge of his nose. He was chuckling lightheartedly, though his facial expression looked thoughtful. Then he muttered the words "I can't," and said that he'd been teasing Waters. How could he be expected to print something that would surely infuriate General Garcia? Paid by Waters, he would be 34,600 pesos richer, but his life would be worth that much less.

Waters called him "a coward, a pitiful mockery of a reporter," and left. He walked back to his room. He stretched out on his bed and opened a bottle of rum. Facing him on the wall was a mirror, and he could see how, since the card game, he had let his appearance go to seed. Thorny black growth had sprouted on his face, his hair was disheveled, and his black pants and gray collared shirt were soiled. He sat up against the wall and took a swig of the liquor. Though harsh, it relaxed him, allowing him to think. Within three days he was supposed to leave the country, but as yet he had made no arrangements to depart. Was that the answer? He could put this episode behind him and sail for Cuba or Monaco or another place where there were casinos. If he could but forget the wrong that had been done him, he could leave this place with twice as fat a bankroll as he'd brought to it. But no sooner had he considered this option than he put it out of his mind, vowing to stay on the island until he collected the debt or avenged himself on General Garcia.

On Thursday morning, under dreary skies, Waters rose from bed and set out for the presidential palace. He was determined to speak with the General and to make a final, courteous plea for the 34,600 pesos. He crossed the capital swiftly, walking between the strolling pedestrians and the people riding horses, but when he got to the corner near the palace, about to turn left and go down the block that led to the building, two men ran up from behind him and grabbed his forearms. Nothing in their olive-dark skin, casual clothes, or scraggly whiskers set them apart from other islanders, but each man had a revolver in his belt. Alarmed, Waters stopped in his tracks. He asked them what they wanted. One of them told him to start walking in the opposite direction. He was of course at liberty to move anywhere he chose in the capital, but he had best keep away from the palace: the General would not be receiving his company again. Waters stared at them a moment, his brow wrinkling, then he forced himself to smile and said that he understood perfectly. He would give them no trouble. The pair observed how calm he looked, indeed how indifferent he appeared, and they let him go. Waters turned to walk away. The men followed him, however, and when Waters glanced back over his shoulder, they waved at him mockingly. He realized they must have been shadowing him since the night of the poker game.

This violation of his privacy, along with the present rebuff, was the final indignity he would permit himself to suffer, and Waters decided then and there to have his revenge on their leader, the President.

Waters returned to his hotel. As he passed through its open doorway, he looked back again. The two security agents were sitting on a park bench across the street, and Waters cursed under his breath at them as he continued walking toward his room. Inside, for the remainder of the morning, he paced the floor. The battle lines had been drawn and now he had to think of a way to get even with Garcia. His problem was unchanging: he could not storm the palace; the army protected Garcia so well he was invulnerable to external attack. But perhaps he could inflict harm on the General's allies, the people who since the night of the game had been taunting and ignoring him. They were acting as if they were the limbs of Hernandez Garcia. They were doing his bidding as if he were the brain that controlled their actions. It sickened Waters, this lack of sincerity they had, and as he dwelled on his image of them, an idea occurred to him. He considered it from various angles. He knew it was a plan born of desperation, but he could not think of a more expedient way to square his accounts. Smiling without joy, yet feeling excited despite himself, he hummed that old Confederate song called "Dixie."

Not much later, Waters emerged from his room. He walked around the garden courtyard to the entranceway of the hotel. From here he saw the two men still sitting in the plaza across the street. He went over to them and they both stood up, their hands on their pistols.

"You men can go home," he said. "I won't try to get the money anymore. I'm beaten and I know it."

Neither of them answered, so he continued. "I'm going into the forest for a hunting trip. I'll be back tomorrow afternoon and catch a boat off the island on Saturday. I'd like to enjoy the wilderness here one last time before I leave."

"You know you can't," said the shorter of the two. "We're to keep you in the city till you go."

"But that's ridiculous. You think I intend to hide in the bush? I'm a person who lives for luxury."

"It's out of the question," the man said. "Our orders come directly from General Garcia."

Waters recalled that the President had told him, after the poker game, to stay out of the forest or else have a price put on his head. Could the hunting he'd done there and the fact that he'd killed birds indigenous to the island have upset Garcia? The General had never spoken of having a special love for animals. If he was a dabbler in zoology, a man who at his core detested hunting, why had he not come out and said so? Waters shook his head, bewildered, and it struck him that the General might think he'd been fraternizing with the enemy, the rebels. Was that possible? He'd never said anything to denigrate the rebels, and he kept riding back and forth between the peasant world and the hacienda world. That alone might elicit Garcia's suspicion. Should he make a last attempt to explain to the General by passing him a message? The General might hold a view of him entirely inaccurate. He did not like that but assured himself that it didn't matter — the General had welshed pure and simple — and he thought once again of his foremost concern. He had to get into the bush to execute his revenge.

"The decision is final?" he said. "I can't go?"

"You can't."

Waters pouted, like a man at wit's end, and trudged back to the hotel. In his room he had thrown together his belongings. His money and clothes lay stuffed in his rucksack, which now he put on, and to the belt around his waist he attached the leather sheath containing his machete. Waters owed four days' rent on his lodgings, and the pesos required to settle this bill he laid down on the table with a note of thanks for the flawless service. He then dashed across the courtyard, his loaded hunting rifle in his right hand. The doors to all the other rooms were closed, and the entire place was quiet for siesta time. The maids and guests were asleep; the dining hall, at one end of the building, was deserted. Waters peeked into the office, next to the hotel's entranceway, and saw behind the desk the proprietor snoring in his chair. He stepped over to the jutting wall adjacent to the main doorway, and from that spot he peered outside. The clouds of the morning had vanished, bands of heat shimmered above the ground. Only the two men were in sight — they had plunked themselves down on the bench again — and both of them looked drowsy. Waters' rifle was an old one, a Winchester 73, but he had used it so often it felt like an extension of his hands. He raised it and took aim. In the blink of an eye, before the men could react, he had fired twice. His shots hit their targets dead on and each man clutched at his shattered left knee, howling and swearing. One groped for his pistol, but Waters shot him in the elbow, disabling his arm. The hotel proprietor now awakened, yelling to the gods above and asking what in heaven's name was going on. He jumped out of his office waving a revolver, but Waters had fled.

Waters ran down the street to the house of the old horse dealer who had been renting him a piebald for his hunting expeditions. The man was sleeping in a woolen hammock suspended from two trees in his yard. Waters kicked him in the leg, rousing him, and while brandishing his rifle said that he needed the piebald at once. He accompanied the terrified man to the barn and helped him saddle the robust creature. Then he mounted. After they had gone back outside, he stared down at the man with a grim, determined countenance.

"Best of luck to ya," he said. "Here's something for him."

From his trousers' pocket he took the money he'd set aside for the piebald, and the horse dealer accepted it. White in the face, his hands trembling, he fumbled though the notes trying to count them, but jerked his head up when Waters spoke again.

"Let General Garcia know I'll be fighting him until he pays me the 34,600 pesos."

What he meant to do in this fight Waters did not say, and as the man tried to form a response, stammering, he rode down the street to the edge of the city.

He was entering the bush to embark upon his private war.

Waters prodded the piebald and it held up well to his goading. He took it on a path north, thundering along the flat hard track, ready to swerve into the bushes if he heard anyone gaining on him. With his rifle strapped to the horse, he told himself he would rather die shooting than surrender to the lackeys the General sent with a directive to capture him. But he heard nothing, no men or horses, no noises at all except for the pounding of the piebald's hooves, and after he had gone a number of miles he became convinced nobody was coming. Relieved, he slowed the horse and loosened his grip on the reins. When they came to a brook, Waters stopped and got down from the saddle so that the animal could drink. It did so, greedily, replenishing itself as the flecks of foam on its coat dried, and for the rest of the trip through the bush, Waters let the horse trot, happy with himself for having escaped, but aware that again he was a fugitive.

By nightfall, he had reached the village he was seeking. He guided the horse past the bamboo huts and over toward a cantina. Dogs approached him, a pack of mangy rawboned mutts, but when they started barking at him, running at his horse then skipping away, he kept calm and said, "Git," raising his voice above their clamor. He knew the dogs in these villages, mongrels with more bark than bite, and sure enough they moved off when he yelled, their growls having become whimpers.

Near the cantina, at a hitching post, he tethered his horse. The heat of the day had begun to fade, and in the sky black was replacing the last red of sunset. Still, in the village, not many people were around, and Waters realized that the men were just now returning from their work in the cane fields, ending their long rides back home after a grueling day in the sun. Not until later, after supper, would the cantina come to life, and so when Waters went inside he decided not to rush anything and asked the man behind the counter if he could get something to eat. The man said he could, a plate of beans and rice. And while a slew of bugs and moths collected around the scattered lanterns, Waters sat alone at a table in the corner, eating his food and drinking rum. He mixed the rum in a glass with guava juice.

Gradually, as he had expected, the bar filled. People asked for whiskey, smoked cigars, set up the domino pieces. But he could not tell whether anyone knew of his troubles in the capital. Nobody made any reference to them. Men he knew here, in their worn overalls and straw hats, talked to him with their customary friendliness, and he supposed they assumed from his rifle and rucksack that he was out on a hunting trip, he the famous oddball gringo able to roam at will on the island and blend with people from every social strata.

It must have been close to ten o'clock when Waters brought up what he'd come to say. He had stayed in the bar longer than he usually did on his visits, and somebody asked him whether he was planning to sleep in the village; riding back toward the capital now might be dangerous owing to bandits. He was at a table with three other men, all of whom were beginning to yawn from their day of work and their night of drinking, and he did not know who could help him in the bar. To buy himself time, he sipped from his drink. He was contemplating how exactly to put the statement he had come to make. Then he said it, in a steady voice, that he wanted a meeting with Raoul Cardenes Amoros. Not wanting to sound crazy, he told everyone that he had once spoken to Amoros in this very cantina, and he said he was making his request in this fashion because he knew of no other way to establish contact with the rebel leader. Someone, he stated, had to know how to deliver a message to the elusive figure, and he was letting it be known that what he had come to say to Amoros were words that man, a great man, would want to hear.

Nobody responded to this pronouncement. Yet Waters felt himself the center of attention. All domino games had stopped, the talking ceased, the man behind the counter froze in the act of pouring fruit wine into a glass. If he had said the sky was falling, nobody has an hour to live, Waters could not have been more effective in silencing the crowded cantina, and he straightened himself in his armless wooden chair to reinforce the impression that he was serious. But judging from the faces on everybody, the staring eyes and inquisitive frowns, no one thought he had been joking.

Waters looked through the clouds of cigar smoke.

"Well? Can anyone help me?"

As if a bell had been rung, a signal made, everyone rose and fled through the door. Everyone except the bartender and a man from a table near the counter, and this man, a squat dark fellow in dusty clothes, ambled over to Waters' table and plopped himself down on a chair. He had eyes that were red with fatigue and whiskey, and while Waters looked at him, waiting for something to be said, the man displayed a guarded smile that showed off his rotting teeth.

"Why do you want to see Amoros?"

"I can't tell you."

"You tell me and I'll report it to him."

"I don't know you. I want to speak to Amoros himself."

"That might not be so easy."

"It's to have a meeting set up. Can we? You tell me how, or where, and I'll be there."

The man got up and went to whisper with the man at the bar. Everybody else had gone. Waters finished his rum while watching the two men talk, and it occurred to him that perhaps they thought he wanted to harm Raoul Amoros. They could be thinking he had been sent by his rich friends in town and promised a handsome sum of money for the elimination of their leader. But did that make sense? To request a meeting with Amoros so he could kill him would be an act of suicide.

The conference over, the thickset man with the yellowing teeth turned from the bar to address him again, and Waters was told that he could get to meet Amoros if he had the patience to wait till morning. As this was not a question of patience for Waters, but of necessity, of having to see Raoul Amoros or else find someone to take him off the island, he said that the morning was fine with him, but where would he sleep tonight? Unless he was mistaken, there were no hotels in the village, and he did not know the residents well enough to call on any for their hospitality. "Sleep here," the man said, "in the cantina," and he looked at the cantina owner to make sure he had his consent. When the owner nodded, giving his permission, the other man made to leave, walking toward the door with hurried steps, and the cantina owner told Waters he would have to sleep on the floor or a table since he had no extra beds.

"Mine's in the back," he said to Waters, "and I'm using that for myself."

Waters opted for a table pushed against two other tables, and the cantina owner gave him a pillow. After snuffing out the lantern and closing the door, the man retired to his back room, separated from the bar by a curtain, and Waters in his dirty clothes and bare feet lay on his back in the perfect darkness listening to the crickets outside. The air had the heaviness that comes before a rainstorm, and in the cantina itself the night's cigar smoke had not been dispersed. A gray cloud in the black of the room, it carried with it a bitter stench, something akin to burning trash. Waters could also smell the odors of the people who'd left, sweat residues from the night's crowd. All of it made breathing unpleasant, and without a mosquito net to use Waters kept feeling insects on him, flies alighting on his unprotected arms, mosquitoes sucking the blood from his feet. This could be his life for a while, he thought, a life in which the going would be rough, and even though he felt ready for the challenge, he found it hard not to think with yearning of his old mansion outside New Orleans.

Though he'd lived alone, he'd seldom been lonely, and because of the ease in his manner he had gotten on well with his two servants. He had treated them both like people, equals almost, and each had possessed a spacious room in the house. Damn, that house and his own room — he remembered everything. He remembered his bed and the lazy mornings he'd spent in it, drinking coffee with milk and cinnamon, eating donuts baked by the cook, reading the papers brought by a rider paid to deliver them from the city. The sheets on that bed were of the finest linen, the pillows sewn from down, and he had surrounded himself with plushness by lining his walls with white velvet and putting a Persian carpet on the floor. That had been his house, abandoned because for one brief moment he had lost control of himself, and in all probability he would never see it again. But this didn't mean he could never have a stately home again; once he had done with General Garcia, he would see to it that he lived in style. He would live in high style in a place of his own because even before he'd taken to the bush in his struggle to get the poker winnings due him, he had grown weary of living in a hotel.

The shrieking of roosters woke him, a shrill intrusion into his dreams. Caught between their calls and his sleep, he needed a minute to find his bearings. Then he recognized where he was, and remembered why he'd bolted from the capital, and he sat up on the table stretching his arms and working the kinks out of his neck. All along his body, from his night on the wood, he felt stiff. But he was wondering, as he limbered up, where he would be meeting Raoul Amoros.

That morning it was hot and clear. Waters felt he had slept soundly. The glistening wetness on the ground told him it had rained during the night, and as he stepped into the puddle-pocked street drying in the intense sun, he saw the men in straw hats taking the path into the bush for another day of work in the fields. Not so the cantina owner, however, standing near the entrance to his place with a mug of steaming coffee in his hands, and when Waters saw that the man had shaved, he asked where he could clean himself up.

"In the river," said the man. "You can wash there. But you don't have to get dressed up for Raoul."

He bathed in the cool green water of the river using the soap the man had given him. He toweled himself off on the bank, changed into a fresh shirt and pants, fastened his belt with the sheathed machete, and walked back to the cantina. The man had boiled water in a pot, and behind the bar, over the pot, gazing into a chunk of mirror as he stroked himself with his razor, Waters removed the scruff from his face. He would have liked to cut his hair, but he contented himself with combing it, smoothing back the long brown locks till they fell in a stylish wave to his shoulders. His sack reloaded, he went outside and attached it to his horse, which the cantina owner, a short time before, had provided with a feed bag, and then Waters asked if he could have breakfast. The man spooned out a lump of black beans. He paid for the food and the horse's grain from the wad of cash in his pocket, dollars and pesos won through poker, and as he thumbed through all his bills, he wondered whether he should hide the money or tell Amoros that he had it. In exchange for what he would ask of Amoros, would Amoros demand the cash from him?

The thickset man from the night before came waddling into the bar and Waters knew the time had come.

"Here?" Waters said.

"No," the man said, and he unrolled a red scarf, saying he would have to use it as a blindfold.

"It's for safety reasons," the man said, as if Waters did not know, and the man tied it on him outside as he was raising his leg to put his foot into the stirrup.

They started off in the viscid heat. Waters surrendered to the strange sensation of riding in darkness while holding the reins, feeling the up and down motion of the horse as it walked along. His escort, who had told him his name was Juan Ramirez, had tied a rope from his own saddle to the pommel on Waters' saddle, and so Waters had to do nothing but keep himself upright on the piebald and duck under the branches and vines Ramirez warned him of in their path. He could tell they were riding uphill for the most part, going through light and shady patches in the fragrant lushness of the highlands. Even though the air cooled somewhat, he perspired heavily under his blindfold. Sometimes Ramirez would speak to him, asking him whether he had family back in the States, telling him that among village people he was still something of a mystery, but in between these stints of talk he was left alone with his thoughts and the sing-song music of the birds in the trees.

It was early afternoon, after they had splashed across a stream, when Waters became aware of voices. They sounded like those belonging to men, a group, and Waters thought they must have arrived at the rebels' camp. From close by came a whistle, louder than the voices, and Ramirez told him to undo the blindfold.

Amoros was the first to greet him, stepping from his men and extending the long bony hand Waters had shaken in the village cantina. Five weeks had gone by since that meeting, and Amoros looked as Waters remembered him — a man with the features of an African and the skin coloring of an almond. He had added no meat to his ascetic frame, and because he was wearing all black again, he appeared taller than he actually was and had that sinister aura about him. And yet there was something feminine too, maybe from how soft his skin looked and how supple, or maybe because he had his hair tied by a ribbon at the back of his neck. That touch, the red ribbon, was the one decorative thing on him, and Waters took it as a sign that this man fighting a war did perhaps have vain points, that he was proud of his crop of hair and its untainted blackness. He seemed, in this aspect, like a dandy in the bush, and in no way did he look ravaged by the defeats he had suffered in his years leading revolts. To all appearances, he was unscarred by the struggle he was waging, and Waters imagined it was partly this, the charisma inherent in his glow and sparkle, that kept drawing supporters to him. The name The Fifty, as his fighters were called, did not reflect their numbers; at this one rebel site there were about thirty men, camped here with their bedrolls and tents, prepared to move with their horses and guns.

Invited by Amoros to sit, Waters found himself in the circle and under the scrutiny of everyone there. He envisioned his father having done this — ate and slept and drank in the forest while fighting a war for survival — but knew that the difference between the Confederates and himself was that they had fought for what they saw as their freedom while he had no stake in the island's fortunes. Amoros and The Fifty wanted to overthrow General Garcia. His objective was revenge for the unpaid debt. Needless to say, he made no mention of his poker with the General while he was talking to Amoros and answering the questions put to him, and he said that the reason he'd asked for this meeting, requested a face to face with Amoros, was because he wanted to tell him that he hoped to join The Fifty and help them fight for their cause.

"You asked me once to join you," he said, "and I told you no. Now I've reconsidered."

"Have you?" Amoros said.

The rebel leader kept asking him questions. Wasn't he an apolitical man? What had made him change his outlook? This island was not his island and the struggle of the peasants not his struggle, and as everyone here among them knew, he played high stakes poker with the island's wealthiest people. From those bastards, through his gambling, he derived his livelihood, and at that last discussion in the bar he had said without equivocation that he wanted to keep playing cards so he could continue living in comfort.

"Life with us isn't easy," said Amoros. "You know that."

Indeed he did, Waters replied, but his time on the island had given him a new perspective. The abuses he'd seen the army commit, the arrogance of the island's wealthy, had made him rethink where he stood. A political conscience was waking in him. He felt guilty fraternizing with the island's rich, and though he knew the perils involved, he wanted to contribute however he could to what was rumored all over the island to be the next big assault by The Fifty.

"You've launched five rebellions in seventeen years," Waters said. "But this time it has to be won."

"That's the idea," Amoros said.

"And let me tell you," Waters went on, "in the capital, the aristocrats, they're scared. They know something big is brewing."

"So you want to be on the winning side? You're jumping ship before theirs goes down?"

"I'm not part of their ship," Waters said. "I've never been part of any ship."

"It's always been you for yourself alone."

"You could say that. But this is different. I've made a choice."

"Johnny Reb the fighter. Is that it?"

"The South lost the war, but its soldiers know how to fight."

With a wry smile, Amoros agreed, lauding the fierceness in his tone, but what he was dying to know about Waters was why the man had ever left the United States. He remembered Waters telling him that he'd done it for a change of scenery, but this explanation seemed lacking. If he'd come for the island's beauty, why should its gross injustices bother him? Even if they had got to him, why should he stay and risk his life fighting when all he had to do to find a better place was go somewhere else in the region? He could find gambling and the glories of nature on an island like Cuba or Martinique.

"And the rich don't control those islands, too?"

"The rich control the world," said Amoros. "The point is, for a man like you, why fight them?"

"Because I'm not what I was," Waters said. "That's what I'm trying to tell you."

He did confess, speaking bluntly, that the reason he'd left the United States was because he had killed a man — "stabbed him in the heart when he tried to cheat at cards" — but he said he could always go back if he wanted to. If not to the New Orleans area, then he could go to parts further west, like California or

Texas. Being a fugitive was a silly reason to avoid the United States of America, giant country that it was, nation in which anyone could hide, and he said yet again that his determination to stay on the island had everything to do with his political awakening and nothing whatsoever to do with his past.

"I killed the man," he said, "because of my strong moral sense. That's something deep, something born in me, that goes well beyond politics."

The cracked, weathered faces stared at him from under bandanas and hats, and among all the men a debate started on the pros and cons of letting him join them. Sunlight cut through the cover of the trees, making the ground they sat on hot, and sitting there in his sweat-moistened clothes without headwear for protection, Waters felt woozy. He was hungry also, his stomach rumbling, and he listened as if in a mild fever dream to the ragged-clothed band going over his merits. Though most of the men seemed in favor of using him, including him in their operations, a man addressed as Commander Iturbide was adamantly opposed to him. Gray-eyed and unshaven, burdened with a paunch, Iturbide took the position that Waters might have come as a spy, hired by his friends among the landowners. Since his previous meeting with Amoros, Waters might have gone back to their enemies, reported on the overture from the rebel leader, and proposed that he be a paid agent. Commander Iturbide, with his skin like ebony, said they should never take an American thinking he could believe in their cause, and it would be an extravagant folly with an American from the South, the Confederate States, the land that had fought a horrible war to save the institution of slavery.

"Not fair," Waters said. "I have nothing against colored people."

"And your parents and grandparents?"

"They owned a plantation."

"With slaves?"

"Naturally."

"That's all you need to say."

Grumbling broke out among the men, skepticism flashing in their eyes. Two or three of the blacks in the circle grabbed hold of their machetes, about to pull them from their horsehide belts. Just like that a hostile feeling seemed to have spread through the group, and Iturbide gave him a look that might have been the glare of a white-eyed snake. Put on the defensive, seeing that he needed a dramatic gesture, Waters decided to throw caution to the wind, and with a jaunty flip of his arm he exhibited the stack of money from his pocket.

"Everything I have," he said. "At your disposal."

Commander Iturbide scoffed, claiming that the money could have come from his backers, the landowners. But among the other fighters, to Waters' relief, the move had a calming effect. They apparently took him at his word that he had handed over his personal wealth. Their eyes softened, smiles formed, the hands gripping the machete handles unclenched and fell back into laps.

"Here is a man who can ride and shoot," Amoros said. "We can use him."

Nevertheless, as if to appease Commander Iturbide and admit that issues were still unsettled, he told the circle that Waters would have to prove himself first. Waters would have to complete an assignment to show the members of The Fifty that he was truly part of their struggle.

"Call it an initiation," he said.

And Waters said, "Whatever you got for me, I'll do."

BLOOD FOR THE GENERAL

On more than one occasion, the General had given express orders not to be disturbed when in his red room. He would tell his aides to hold their reports until he was finished with his pleasures and had returned to his office. In the red room, the room with walls the color of blood, he escaped from the cares of power and lost himself in the flesh of virgins. He had them brought to him, had them selected from his team of connoisseurs who scoured the countryside for girls, and if he liked a new girl's looks when they displayed her to him in the palace, she was given a meal and a bath and then fitted out for a peignoir by a palace tailor. They had a batch of peignoirs stored in a closet and the tailor would alter whichever sheath best showed off the girl's attractions. Sometimes, at the General's command, she would be supplied with black stockings and high heeled slippers. A beauty expert would touch up her face and somebody else might style her hair, and depending on the mood the General was in and the fragrance he wanted to savor, the attendants would apply perfume to her body or light a stick of incense in the room. Elaborate preparations, which his aides deemed excessive for breaking in a virgin, but he did not want to be a brute. He had his standards and propriety. He preferred to see the girls naked after he went through the rapture of disrobing them. And so long as he was the leader of this country, so long as he controlled the treasury, there would be on his governmental staff a crew of tailors and beauticians entrusted with the job of making sure the virgins brought to him at the palace looked as ripe and alluring as possible.

He never did them harm, but he loved their blood. It was for their blood he insisted on virgins, and would warn the families he took the girls from that they had better be unsullied or there would be hell to pay. On the other hand, for all those girls delivered to him so he could enjoy them in the red room's bed and lick their blood, there was strictly the royal treatment for the duration of their palace stay.

His chef would prepare that first meal for them, a lady maid would see to each girl as she took her bath in rose-scented water, and when Garcia had finished with the girls, they would be fed and bathed again and rewarded with money to take home to their families. Without exception they came from poor families, peasants living in their shacks in the south, and what he gave the fathers for the use of their daughters equaled what they earned in a year. Or two years. So who could complain? A family's daughter would lose her virginity and might be difficult to marry off later, but into the bargain came the money for the family to improve its lot in life. That was no mean benefit, and a family could say (with pride, he hoped) that their daughter had been among the girls chosen to visit the General's red room. A father could say she'd served the republic and sacrificed her maidenhood so that the General could have her blood and continue to live in good health.

Yes, virgins' blood is what kept him young. It kept him vigorous. He fully believed in its restorative properties, and that was why when engaged in the red room, his time spent with the virgins took on weight and consequence. Possessing the virgins was a rite essential to his well-being and those who distracted him during this rite knew they would face his anger.

Despite that, his aides would interrupt him when they felt they had to. And that seemed to be the case today. General Garcia had a girl in bed with him, undressed and lying on her back, looking at him with apprehensive eyes, when someone came walking up the hall with boot heels clicking on the marble tiles. About to roll over onto the girl and start the act that would draw her blood, the General reined in his desire and waited to hear what was so urgent, and after a fist banged on the door, a resonant voice announced itself.

"Yes, Colonel Bosch?"

"Excuse the interruption."

"You know I'm busy, Colonel Bosch."

"It's something I think you should know, General."

"What is it?"

"Bad news."

"How bad?"

"The gringo. The American, Jack Waters."

But hearing that name was sufficient for the General, he did not want to listen to anything else, and he told the colonel they could talk in his office when he'd completed his work in the red room.

"General, sir…"

"Later, Colonel Bosch, later."

How dire could it be? What could it be? That gringo who had beaten him in poker carried himself with a haughty air, but whatever he had to hear about the gentleman could wait until he deflowered this girl.

No older than fifteen (his minimum age for girls was twelve), she had tawny-brown skin and hands not yet ruined by work. She lay stock-still as he kissed her nipples and ran his hands over her body. Everything on her was taut but pliant, with the elasticity of youth, and the General felt his excitement mounting when he saw that she kept her eyes open. So many, in their fright, would close their eyes or look away or raise their arms to cover their eyes. But this young girl with her lustrous black hair kept her gaze pinned on him as if to learn from what he was doing. She finally shut her eyes when it was over and he had licked her blood off the sheets. Though she bit down on her lower lip, no tears appeared on her face. This too marked her as a rarity — most girls curled up and cried — and the General smiled with respect. He said she had a toughness beyond her age and would no doubt find herself a husband, and he told her she could have the use of the palace until his men returned her by horseback to her village in the south.

"You've served your President, and this republic. Your family will be well-rewarded."

Invigorated, refreshed, pleased with the taste of the girl's blood, he still did not feel like seeing Colonel Bosch and talking to him about the American. So he stayed in bed, resting himself on the bloodied sheets and peering up at the ceiling mirror reflecting his pale, rotund image, and he imagined himself in a different era, ruling as a king in an earlier time. Then he would have had even vaster power than what he had as president here, and he would have had all pleasures for the taking. Like the Roman emperors. They'd been able to satisfy their appetites without fear of petty censure. They had whole courts dedicated to pleasure, while he had men like Colonel Bosch, intent only on affairs of state, the health and security of the regime. But what good was being president, Garcia wondered, if he could not enjoy the fruits it bestowed, the treats it allowed him to procure? If he wanted champagne shipped from France, he got it; if he wanted Swiss chocolate or prime cuts of beef sent from Argentina, they were his. Everything else, the administrative part, was vexing.

The girl left the room in the charge of a maid. She was wrapped in a pink silk robe, clattering along in thin-heeled slippers. The maid had readied a bath for her, and the thought of washing and getting out of bed reminded Garcia that he had business waiting. It was time to put on his ruler's face and see what news Colonel Bosch had for him regarding this pest of an American, but the General made no effort at rushing as he rang for another of his servants and had the tub in his bathroom filled. Stepping into the water, which felt lukewarm, he called for matches and a cigar, a Havana from the box in his office, and once he was alone in the sunlit room, he puffed away in a bliss of sweet smoke while reading a book translated from Latin on the lives of the later Caesars.

Bosch, narrow-lipped, clean-shaven, sitting with rigid posture in a chair, saluted him when he got to his office. But he did this without standing up, sending a rude message. He was wearing his full colonel's uniform, the blue-green outfit with all the stripes, as well as his boots and peaked cap, and the sardonic glint he had in his eye seemed to reproach the General's clothes. Garcia had put on light gray pants, oxford shoes, and a short-sleeved white cotton shirt. When out in public, making a speech or touring the island, Garcia dressed formally, in the attire befitting his status, but he did not wear such clothes in the palace unless he was meeting with someone important, a landowner or foreign dignitary. Among his aides, whom he saw every day, he liked to stick to civilian garb and so be cooler in the daily heat, but Colonel Bosch seemed not to mind sweating or having his collar buttoned tight. This was a man capable but prissy, and a man who could get impertinent with him, and the General made a mental note to pay close heed to Bosch from now on.

"What are your aspirations, Bosch?"

"General?"

"When was the last time you had a woman?

"Sir?"

"You heard me."

Garcia had an office furnished with a mahogany desk and two black, rock-solid chairs left behind by the last Spanish governor. The office also functioned as his library, and the shelves along the walls contained his books on the history of ancient Rome. One large window facing west let in the light and allowed him to watch evening sunsets, and set up neatly in a row on his desk were the boxes crammed with deluxe cigars imported from throughout the Americas. He felt he might like another smoke now, maybe a gentle Brazilian cigar, but he wanted to have it alone and in peace, not with the colonel staring at him. Bosch had no vices as far as he knew, sustaining what he termed his inner strength through his regular attendance at church.

"You're not answering my questions, Bosch."

"It's not what I came here to discuss."

"We'll get to the American. But after you humor me with answers."

"Sir? I won't."

"About women. Let's start there. Have you ever been with one?"

"I'm married, General."

"I mean other than your wife."

"My wife and I took a sacred vow. I don't want other women."

There you had it, the pious colonel tucking in his chin and stiffening his lips. He squirmed and fidgeted in his chair. General Garcia, using his fingers, began to eat the avocado he had lying before him on a dish. Someone from the kitchen had put it on his desk while he was in the bath, and the person had seasoned it right. Sliced in half, sprinkled with pepper and olive oil, an avocado was his favorite snack after fornication in the red room.

"All right, Colonel Bosch. What about the American?"

Bosch explained. And since he had laid the groundwork by saying the news about Waters was bad, Garcia Napoles only rolled his eyes on hearing that the gringo had shot the two men assigned to watch and follow him.

"Did they get him, too?" the General asked, and knew right away that they had not, since Bosch let out a sigh before answering.

The General held up a hand for silence. Did he have to hear more? Twenty minutes ago, after his bath, he had felt light enough to levitate, but in his position something invariably arose to drag one down to earth. Resigned to having his day spoiled, he signaled Colonel Bosch to go on, but he consoled himself as he listened to the story with the taste of his avocado, smooth as whipped butter in his mouth.

"So he's disappeared," Bosch said, concluding. "And we can take that to mean he's somewhere with the rebels."

The men shot by Waters had been tended by doctors who said they might never walk again, and the horse dealer who said that Waters had come to his stable and taken a horse from him at gunpoint had been arrested and put in jail pending the General's decision on him. But Garcia ordered that he be released — the man was of no significance — and said that the pair who had failed in their mission could be left free also; being crippled would be their punishment. As for Waters, flushed out of his duplicitous mode and made to show his true rebel colors, that man would have to be caught, but Garcia wanted him taken alive so he could talk to him again.

"We'll see how arrogant he is with nails in his balls."

He said good day to Bosch, finished eating his avocado, licked off his fingers, and lit a Brazilian cigar. As the smoke in the room accumulated, he sank down in his cushioned seat and gave the escape of the gringo thought. What he found baffling was why an American would help the rebel forces on his island, when he and his regime were open and cooperative with the American government. American companies had carte blanche to come down here and do business, and once a year in January, American troops and his own conducted joint exercises on the island's southern coast. This man then, Waters, had to be some sort of fanatic, a political ideologue, but the General still found it bizarre that an American from the South would be here helping the rebels and the black-skinned people in their ranks. Garcia knew enough about the United States to know about slavery and the Civil War and the creation of the Ku Klux Klan, and so this man Jack Waters did not conform to his idea of a child of the Confederacy. Was he himself black? Or of mixed blood? Waters had a sandy skin tone. He gave Waters credit for being clever, for having charmed the landowners until they figured him out, but the General could feel himself getting angry as he thought about Waters beating him. Waters had won the poker game, and had been smug afterwards. The gringo hadn't cheated; he had undeniable expertise. But Garcia hated to lose in anything, and insult was added to injury when he lost at cards to a gringo.

The next morning, back in his office, having received no word on Waters' location, the General decided it would be prudent to have a talk with the United States ambassador. He did not relish a talk, but the sad truth was he had little choice. Waters, regardless of his political loyalties, was an American citizen, and any time there was a legal complication for an American on the island, the ambassador wanted to be informed. If Garcia had his men capture Jack Waters and throw him into a jail cell, the news might reach the ambassador somehow, and there could be ugly repercussions. The ambassador would feel that the General had overstepped his bounds by not consulting him first, and a tension Garcia did not need or want could hurt his relationship with Washington.

Accordingly, before sitting down to lunch, Garcia dispatched a messenger to summon the ambassador to the palace. He told the man to bring back a reply from the ambassador, and though he got one, a sheet of paper with the word "Pronto" written on it, nothing else, the General knew it might be early evening by the time the American diplomat showed up. The sluggard would have his lunch, including French or Italian wine, take his siesta, bathe, hit the rum, and then saunter over from the embassy mansion since he couldn't ride a horse when tipsy. Ambassador Sanford Paulsen III, from Vermont, had been born to a Methodist father who repaired clocks for a living and preached the value of punctuality, but his sun-soaked years in the tropics, four years posted in Guatemala and five in Martinique, had eroded his memory of his father's sermons.

This evening, he was true to expectation. The palace clocks had just tolled six, and Garcia himself had napped and bathed, when a servant knocked on his office door and said that Paulsen was waiting in the anteroom. Garcia instructed that he be shown in. Not even his opening of the office window provided adequate ventilation against the fumes that entered with Paulsen. He was dressed in a blue linen suit, well-pressed and not without dash, but he emitted a scent so strong it made Garcia think he slept in a wine vat.

"Ambassador."

"General."

Garcia noticed that even speaking Spanish, Paulsen never slurred his words. He had unclouded eyes, but he had that odor clinging to him and a discoloration in his skin, a yellowish tinge in his face and hands that must have been due to an unhealthy liver. To Garcia, he was a man who had given up on life, who did not care if he drank himself to death. After his years in Guatemala and Martinique, he had been expecting a post in Rome or Paris, and when Washington had sent him here, he'd told everyone he met that he was sick and tired of the tropics.

"They may as well have sent me to Devil's Island," he liked to say.

His reaction to the story about Jack Waters was a muted one. He raised and lowered his thin gray eyebrows and put a tobacco-stained finger to his lips.

One might have thought he was feigning interest and thinking instead of his next drink, but then he asked with real pique why he'd heard nothing of this man, a man who had been on the island for months. That an American would come here and give aid to the rebels did not astonish him — "The United States has its madmen" — but he did share the General's view that Jack Waters was an anomaly for a man born in the South. And since the General made no allusion to his poker game with Waters or the debt on which he'd welshed, Ambassador Paulsen never considered that the activities of Jack Waters might have their roots in something personal. As he put it, Waters was indeed a political radical, or he was a man for hire, a mercenary.

"Do you think you can find out anything about him?" the General said. "I'd like to know."

"Why?"

"Because, Ambassador, he may be connected to people in your country sending money to the rebels here."

"I haven't heard of anything."

"You wouldn't, sleeping in your hammock and drinking the French wine I send you. But we have enemies on this island, and I'm the one who's got to crush them. So maybe you can do your work for a change."

Wounded, but without the fortitude to argue, Ambassador Paulsen went red in the face. He said he would do what he could. General Garcia smiled to himself and saw the man out of his office, watching as a servant in a black and white uniform escorted Paulsen down the hall and toward the palace exit. Garcia had chided him deliberately, but he thought the ploy would pay dividends later, when Paulsen arrived back at the embassy and spoke to his wife about the meeting. In the meantime, however, Paulsen was humiliated, and the diplomat strode through the palace gate with piercing bitterness in his heart. Here he was, an American in the State Department, with extensive experience and a fluency in languages — French, Spanish, Italian — and he was compelled because of etiquette to let himself be disparaged by an insufferable tin-pot president, dictator of a speck in the ocean.

Craving lubrication, heavy with his feeling of self-pity, the ambassador made off through town. Roosters were pecking at crumbs in the streets, laundry hung slack from long lines, stray cats and dogs roamed everywhere. Paulsen could smell their droppings, which steamed in the heat, and the soapy water running in gutters leading away from the courtyard wells. In every crack in the cobble-paved streets flora grew red, green, and purple, and because the day had been so dry grit was rising from the dirt roads, rising and clumping, floating in the air, submerging everything in a brownish haze. Tonight it would rain and the air would be cleared, and tomorrow would dawn bright and dewy and another day on the island would pass in which he would sleep, swat at flies, bathe twice, and drink. A day like every other day here, monotonous and stifling, empty of entertainment or culture. All you had here were the casinos, and since he was not a gambling man, that didn't leave him much to do. Compared to Martinique even, the island was dead. Martinique had the spice of French culture to enliven it, and the town of Saint Pierre, until the eruption of Mount Pelee, had boasted of having an opera house. He adored opera, and one reason he'd been hoping for a European posting was so he could go to the opera houses there: La Scala, Bayreuth, the Paris Opera. Stuck in Central America and then the French Antilles, he had diverted himself by imagining what it would be like in that rarified sphere, a sphere of champagne and society balls, of princesses and nobleman. You did have aristocrats here, too, but to Paulsen they seemed a different breed. They were New World rich, families that had made their fortunes through slave-harvested sugar. To him there was a patina of barbarism associated with the Americas, and what he sought was refinement, the glitter of a walk along the Seine before an evening of Puccini.

Halfway back to the embassy mansion, the ambassador stopped off at an inn. It had a bar in the front and he asked for a glass of dark rum. As he drank, the black barman kept smirking at him. The ambassador could guess why. Everyone on this island knew that his wife took lovers right under his nose. This was something else he had to live with; in a country where men were expected to lord over their wives and a wife's adultery, when discovered, more often than not led to murder, he could be nothing but a target of scorn. By being such, he comprehended, he was not doing the United States justice, representing his nation with dignity, but whenever he broached the subject with Isobel, she would fling back her head and laugh.

"Give up young men for our flag?" she would say.

"Yes," he would answer. "You're disgracing it."

"And how do you do your patriotic duty by getting drunk all the time?"

She was at home when he got back, dressed in trousers and a smoking jacket, playing her piano in the evening breeze wafting in off the bay. When they'd first come to the island to replace his predecessor and take up residence there, Isobel had said without hesitation which room she wanted for her piano. She was beguiled by the prospect of having a room where she could sit facing the sea and open up the French windows to smell the salt-sea air. The room also had a chaise lounge, chairs, and a white carpet in the center of the floor, and the French windows with their white curtains swung outward onto a veranda commanding a view of the U-shaped harbor. During idle daydreams, standing on the veranda with a glass of French red, Paulsen would at times see himself donning a fake beard and mustache and stowing away on a boat in the harbor, but then he would come to his senses again and tell himself that would be preposterous. Escape from the island could be done without subterfuge; to leave he could resign his post. But that too would mean a washing away of all the years of diligent service he had given to the State Department. Did he deserve that? He had put in his time in Washington and Guatemala and Martinique, and he should not have to end his career ingloriously.

Isobel stopped playing. She was sitting at the keyboard with her hands on the keys and her back straight, her mind on the Mozart sonata she had gone through. At rest like this she was lovely, a forty-two year old woman with sun-burnished skin and reddish-brown hair and a hint of seductive hauteur in her face, and she was not tarnished in the slightest degree by the male clothes she liked to wear. Her wardrobe of pants and smoking jackets caused discussion wherever she went and would pull the flocks of young men to her. What they admired was her forceful personality and her considerable intellect. She had been given tutors as a child and then been sent to school in England, and she could hold forth on music, philosophy world affairs, literature. These days, she was starting to work on a novel. *Why not?* she'd told her husband. She had always wanted to write. And on this island, where they had an abundance of free time, she had the ideal chance to begin, to compose a book that would draw upon their last ten years living in the tropics. To her it hadn't been ten years of waste but ten years of interest and adventure.

"What's wrong, Sanford?"

She could see it in his eyes, that something was distressing him. And here is where the General's ploy of denigrating Paulsen came into effect: the ambassador, still feeling the bruises from Garcia's verbal lashing, told his wife everything about the palace meeting. He had, he said, been struck to the quick by Garcia's criticisms, and he did not feel under any circumstances that he should have to tolerate them. His wife, however, as Garcia had foreseen, expended no air commiserating with him, and she suggested he silence the General by doing what Garcia asked, the work he was supposed to do in his role as American ambassador.

"Why do you think you didn't get a post in Europe?"

"Why?

"Because of shoddy work in Martinique."

"Who told you that?"

"It's common knowledge, Sanford."

And knowledge that sent Sanford reeling, weakened him in his knees and ankles and made him slump into a chair. Low in the sky, beyond the French windows and the veranda, the sun was a disk of golden fire about to sink into the sea for the night, and Paulsen in another gush of self-pity contemplated running straight out and diving head first off the veranda, letting the sea's dark waters take him.

"I had no idea."

Isobel snorted.

"How could I know if no one tells me?"

"You might see what's going on if you drank less."

"Like about this American?" Paulsen asked. "Jack Waters. Have you heard of him?"

Isobel had, from friends of hers in the wealthy set, and she expressed incredulity that her husband had not. Everyone was talking about Jack Waters and how he'd joined the rebels in the highlands. He had become an infamous name referred to with hatred by people, but she herself thought that everyone might be misreading Waters' character.

"What would you call him?" Paulsen asked. "He's an agitator."

"Or a man angry over a debt."

"What debt?"

"General Garcia didn't tell you?"

Paulsen said no. He knew nothing of a debt. And so it was that his wife then related the story of Waters, Garcia, and the poker game as it had been told to her by someone who knew the landowner who had played in the game. But while everyone else had concluded that Waters was a sly revolutionist, a man who had won money playing cards and sent that money on to the rebels, she herself was not so certain. She had no proof of anything and had never once met Jack Waters, but from the descriptions of him she'd heard, she surmised he could be a professional gambler, a man enraged at the General for his refusal to pay his debt.

"This could be something purely personal. Not political."

"But he was visiting the bush well before the card game with the General."

"To hunt, he would always say, and because he likes it there."

"Who says that?"

"Everyone who knows him."

"But they didn't believe him."

"They came to suspect he was up to something. But ask for specifics and no one has evidence he was working for the rebels. It's all gossip."

Paulsen could tell he would have to make inquiries, find out what he could about Jack Waters and his past, and in his throat he felt the dryness that meant he needed another drink.

"Can you play something for me?" he asked his wife. "Like before? Like you would in the old days?"

Born in Manhattan, she had come to the marriage

with inherited money and connections to New York society. She had been drawn to his passion for music and his ambition to succeed in the diplomatic corps. So how had he let himself disintegrate since? Why had he fallen apart in the tropics? Isobel did not hate him for it, but something worse — felt sorry for him — and as his deterioration continued she was thriving in these backwater places, doing her writing, taking lovers, reveling in the colors and smells of the Caribbean.

"I'm going out later," she said, "and I have to get dressed. But I'll play, let me see…"

Against the backdrop of blackening sky, she plunged into Beethoven, a sonata. *The Pathetique.* She knew it by heart.

WATERS WITH THE REBELS

A bank of mist over the cane field caught the silvery light from the moon. It made everything glow like phosphorus. The sugar cane stalks looked lime-green; the stone crown of the rum-making works, off to the left, might have been a castle built on a mountain obscured by clouds. But this was not a mountain with a castle, it was the island, and Waters on his sturdy black and white horse scanned the rum plantation below and knew the time to prove himself was here. He had suggested the raid to Amoros, telling him he could do it with four, maybe three, if as usual the fog came down and collected in the valley filled by the hacienda. And Amoros, despite the objections of Commander Iturbide, had taken him up on the idea, given him the full allotment of four. He'd told the men to listen to Waters, since for the purposes of this raid he was to be their leader.

"He knows the plantation. He knows the house. Follow his orders."

And they had. There had been no friction between them, the four on their own steadfast horses letting him lead the ride through the bush. From its edge, the summit of a hill, they were facing east and looking straight down into the valley. Guards were down there in that mist, dozing probably, or drunk, and in the plantation's main house six of Waters' old poker friends had their Saturday game going. As Waters saw it, considering this fog, he and his four could slide in, rob the game, and slide out. Then they would race off into the bush, riding hard on the trails, and back at camp he would slap down the money, his initiatory assignment complete.

"Are we ready?"

The four had their horses in a line behind him, holding their rifles, straw hats on their heads, dressed in the tattered gray-olive clothes that blended well with the fog. Waters wheeled his horse around to start it cantering down the slope.

"Everyone stay behind me."

Had his father done this? Led roving troops in raids against the Yankees? He was like those men now, a Confederate fighting, attacking in the night, except he had for help behind him Spanish-speaking men colored shades of brown. He found it funny, thinking about it, that he should be here leading such a group, but then they were down among the cane stalks and all sense of fun dissolved. The coolness of the mist enveloped them and he felt sweat breaking out on his face, sticking to him in cold drops.

"No noise," he said. "Not a whisper."

They stayed behind him, arranged in a file. Bullfrogs were bellowing somewhere close, and the horses' hooves made clip-clop sounds as they walked across the field. The guards, he knew, would be at the house, on the veranda, expecting nothing to happen in the fog, and Waters wanted to be right on them, up at the house, before making the final rush and storming the place for the cash inside. He could already hear their voices, laughter and talk that carried through the fog. And up ahead beyond the stalks he could see the main house, a gigantic distorted baroque shape in the strands of stagnant whiteness. For an instant, no more than a second, Waters felt a pang of loss for the life he'd left behind, not just here but back home, in Louisiana, where he'd had his own estate, his own mansion, the house where he had been the host for his exhilarating card games, but then he blocked the past from his mind and returned his attention to the here and now, this cane field on this hacienda, pulling up his horse when he came to the clearing that began at the end of the cane field. He dismounted, tied the horse to a stalk, and with a single rapid gesture directed the others to do the same.

They did, never letting go of their rifles, not uttering a word. Waters spun round then and took off running while the others leapt into movement and followed him across the clearing. He felt his heart thumping away as he moved through the wet cool fog and got closer and closer to the voices, to the lights shining in the house, but at the steps all thinking stopped and with it his trepidation vanished. He became pure action, an attacker in motion, doing what he'd gone over in his head while back at the camp with Amoros, and the others did not hesitate either, fanning out with lightning speed to disarm the guards stationed on the porch.

As Waters had thought, they were relaxing, two perched on stools at a table playing dominoes and another lying barefoot in a hammock. Waters went for the man in the hammock, springing right and snatching away the rifle the man had balanced on his stomach, pressing the muzzle of his Winchester up against the man's forehead. Then he flung the man's rifle back, off the porch and into the mist.

"You got them?"

He cast a glance across the porch and saw that his companions had done their job. They had their rifles aimed at the domino players.

"All they have is pistols. No rifles."

"Tell them to lay them down slowly," Waters said. "Nice and quiet. No noise."

Waters kept his eye on the man in the hammock, staring down at the dark gawking face, the eyes red-veined from sleep interrupted. He was wearing khakis, his military uniform, and all of a sudden Waters could see that the guard was a boy, seventeen if he was lucky, his cheeks and jaw outlined by fuzz.

"The army takes them early, don't they?"

"We have two kids over here, too."

"Why don't you three get up slow and walk inside the dining room? They should be playing poker right now."

"Mr. Waters…"

"You recognize me? My name precedes me? Isn't that something."

"I don't think you want…"

"Get up and inside," Waters said. "Move."

He dug the Winchester's muzzle into the young guard's neck. Soon all three had risen, lining up in a row as Waters ordered, and Waters and his four frog-marched them through the foyer. They went down a hall lit by a lantern and on into the dining room. Here at a vast circular table covered by a white cloth, six of Waters' old landowner friends had their poker game going. Dressed informally, with short-sleeved shirts open at the collar, they were in the middle of a seven card game, stud poker, with three cards up so far and two down, and each had piles of cash before him.

"Didn't I tell you?" Waters said. "About the stakes? Pretty big."

He told the guards to lie flat on the floor, with their faces to the wood, and not to dare move a muscle. While his helpers stood watch over everyone, pointing their guns at the guards and players, Waters said hello to the players and asked them about their health.

"Doing well I take it? And business is good? That's good."

But he was talking to himself really, because the six with their graying hairs and their disdainful, rum-flushed faces refused to say anything to him. One had his pipe smoking in his hand, another a cigar between his fingers. All had locked into attitudes jut-jawed in their silent contempt, as if they believed his appearance an illusion, something perhaps their collective minds, fearful of Waters and the Amoros rebels, had dreamed into visibility. But if they fought the temptation to believe, stayed still and did not panic, this manifestation of their fears would be gone quick as it had come, one minute there, one minute not, and everything would return to normal. The scare would be over, someone would joke about it, and they would be able to get on with their game.

"Don't wanna talk to me?" Waters said. "Think I'll go away if you do that? No such luck."

He snapped his fingers and the rebel on his right slung a burlap sack off his shoulder. The man went from player to player, round the table, scooping the money into the bag.

"Nobody move."

But no one did, and when the man had all the cash, he tied the mouth of the sack with a string.

"That does it."

"Good," Waters said. "Well done."

"Should we go?"

"You and the others. I'll meet you outside by the horses."

"Why? Is there a problem?"

"No problem. Get going."

So they went, his four companions, running down the hall, and Waters drew the hammer on his rifle. Nobody in the dining room stirred.

"I have a message for the President," he said. "He still owes me $34,600 pesos."

Then he left too, bolting from the room, but as he ran away down the hall, he plucked down the lantern burning on a shelf. It took little time to pause in the foyer and smash the lantern with his rifle butt. Oil splattered, and before stepping out onto the porch, he lit the gray window curtain on fire. The gossamer fabric ignited, flames shooting up along the wall, and Waters tossed the candle from the broken lantern back into a pool of the spilled oil. That caused an explosion of flames, but outside on the porch he stopped again, putting both hands on his rifle. He waited. Inside there were tongues of fire and smoke, but he waited there facing back through the door till the first of the guards came into his sight, scrambling out from the dining room. The man was unarmed and coughing and swearing, and Waters shot at him to wound. He aimed for his leg. The bullet caught his thigh but the man didn't fall; he kept on coming toward the flames, and Waters was forced to shoot again, trying now for his shoulder. That worked. The man fell forward and the two guards behind him ducked down to the floor. Nowhere in view were the landowners, though, as if they might have remained at their table, still reluctant to believe this was happening, and with the flames in the foyer spreading, Waters turned and ran across the grass.

The four others, on their mounts, had his horse untied and ready.

"Let's move," Waters said. "Good job."

And he smiled, while the others smiled, and through the fog white as smoke hovering over the sugar cane field they went galloping toward the hill rising up to the bush. Above them was the moon, silver and full, lighting their way despite the mist, and once as he looked back over the cane field Waters saw the fire through the haze. Red-orange flames were tearing at the mansion. He could even hear above the horses' hooves the men back there who were shouting. Yet not one came in pursuit, and when he was at the top of the hill, about to enter the bush again, Waters took a last look down and saw some figures moving in the mist, tiny figures near the flames, dashing around, carrying things.

"I did it," he said in a soft voice. "I damn sure did it."

He could feel relief setting in, a lightening inside himself. And he knew that his father, if he were alive, would have been proud of him, would have seen him as a genuine heir. Until the day she died, sane but embittered, his mother had told him stories of the man who was Harris Waters, Colonel Harris Waters who had led his own troop fighting the Yankees till his death at Shiloh. She had described over and over the qualities that distinguished him, the strength and valor in his character, his ability to lead men in battle and make them feel invincible. Every man in his troop, of those she met when they came to the house, had attested to his composure under fire; he had been renowned for his marksmanship, be it with a pistol or rifle. To be like him, to live up to his memory, Waters had begun learning to shoot around the time of his ninth birthday, and his mother had encouraged him to practice so he would have the capacity to fight for himself if wronged. She too would have taken pride in having a son lead the raid tonight. With eyes acclimated to the moonlit darkness, the party rode with ease on the vine-hung trails, and Waters felt like he was skimming the earth, flying through the air, his mount a horse with wings like Pegasus.

When they got back to the camp, however, his mood changed. He was expecting acclaim for a job that had brought the rebels funds for ammunition, but as soon as his helpers got off their horses and gave the sack of money to the group, there were suspicions raised about him. A fire was going and the men had been lying around in their bedrolls, waiting to see if he and the others would return, and they did all jump up smiling when he and the four raiders rode up. Amoros came over to him, thin, almond-colored Amoros, dressed in his typical funereal black, hair mussed and hanging to his neck, and when he saw the burlap sack, the reaction he had was joyous.

"I would kiss you, Waters," he said. "If you were a woman."

But then a man who had been on the raid talked. Amoros and his men listened. The man explained how after the robbery Waters had spent time alone with the landowners. Instead of coming out with them to the horses, he had stayed behind momentarily, and they hadn't heard what he said in that dining room.

Whatever it was, it must have been vital, or he would not have delayed his escape, but it seemed he had taken an unnecessary risk in trying to cover nine people by himself.

"Unless it wasn't a risk," someone said, and even before turning to look, even before he'd seen the face black and mistrustful in the firelight, Waters knew the speaker was Iturbide. Commander Iturbide continued to oppose him. And he wouldn't use Waters' name when addressing him; Iturbide called him Dixie.

"You used to own slaves, Dixie. You can't fight with us."

"I've never owned a slave in my life."

"But you would have. If you were born earlier,"

"I'm here and I'm helping. That's it."

But *that* was never it for Iturbide. Whenever he could he did something to make Waters uncomfortable, to put Waters under the gun, and Waters felt as if the man's ill will might become violent. Regardless of what he did with the rebels, what he did to prove himself to them, Iturbide might shoot him one day. Or one night when he was asleep in his bedroll, Iturbide might slit his throat. Iturbide hated him (or hated all Americans or hated all Americans he saw as white) and Waters thought with a sinking feeling that he might have to strike at Iturbide before Iturbide struck at him. That would be murder, no mere squaring of accounts like when he'd stabbed the welsher in New Orleans or the cheater at his house, but Waters could see nothing for it. What was the alternative? Sitting by, doing nothing, and letting the man kill him?

"I have something to show you," Iturbide said.

"Show away," Waters answered. "Where is it?"

"If our commander says yes."

"Why wouldn't I?" Amoros said.

"Then follow me, Dixie. I'll show you what we do to people when we have to."

Despite the dark, Iturbide led Waters through brush and down a snake-narrow path. Waters hadn't noticed the trail before. It opened onto a space around a tree, and beside a torch stuck in the ground, Waters saw a man under ropes, binding him to the tree. Arms at his sides, feet together, he stood with his back against the tree trunk, immobilized by the constraints around his ankles, his midriff and arms, his neck. He was short and black-haired, clothed in garments that resembled rags. He looked unconscious, his face battered and misshapen. Dried blood caked his chin and mouth, mixing with sweat, luring flies. Waters could hear the insects buzzing. They had clustered on the man's left hand, too, the locus of a wound, a cut seeping blood, what Waters noted on further inspection could not be only a cut.

"If you want to know what we do to traitors."

The man was missing four fingers, which lay in the flamelight, at his feet.

"You do this?" Waters said.

"This," answered Iturbide.

"He's been a spy for the landowners," Amoros said, and Waters turned toward the rebel commander, who had entered the open area.

"How did you expose him?"

"Does it matter? We caught him."

"He's breathing," Waters said.

"And so?" said Iturbide.

"If you're done with him, you should end it. Put a bullet through his head."

Amoros smiled but gave no rejoinder, and Iturbide stood studying Waters with a look that defied him to say more. He stared at Waters as if his eyes would force him to spit out a truth, the admission that he was a spy himself. But Waters went to his poker face, blankness incarnate, and didn't volunteer another syllable.

Amoros said they should go back to the others.

Waters had no trouble, in this instance, dispelling the suspicions that were levelled at him. They came from a handful of men, and all it took to dissipate the tension was a reminder that on the raid he had set the mansion on fire and shot a guard pursuing them. Then he said he'd known it was risky dallying in the kitchen with the landowners, but he had done it anyway because he'd wanted to crow at them.

"Childish," he said. "All right. But I did it fast."

"Why when we weren't there?" someone said.

"I don't know. Embarrassment."

"Did you have to do that?"

"I couldn't hold back. Remember, I used to be friends with those people."

Amoros bought the explanation and most everybody else seemed to also (though Iturbide, glowering at him, walked away), and Waters mustered up the courage to ask if there was any rum around. He could use a drink. Somebody handed him a bottle and he went to sit alone by the fire, and while Amoros, surrounded by his men, stooped on one knee and opened the sack and began counting the cash inside, Waters felt his blood heat up. The rum was coursing through him. He wondered whether the men back there, at the mansion, would relay his message to the President. Garcia owed him the 34,600 pesos, and the man had to be made to know the consequences for welshing.

Waters seemed to bring the rebels good fortune. He asked to be included in all their raids, and over the next several weeks, with Waters in tow, they scored a string of successes. They robbed and burned the mansion of Roberto Montoya, a former friend of Waters, attacked an army depot outside the capital, killing soldiers, grabbing weapons, and then razing the depot with dynamite, and they intercepted a shipment of money that was being sent to an army barracks so the soldiers there could be paid.

Out in the harbor, one starless night, Amoros and Waters and two other men took a rowboat over to a ship loaded with casks of rum for export, and under the noses of the sleeping crew they crept down into the cargo hold and pried open the wooden barrels. As the rum streamed out, Amoros lit a stick of dynamite with a fuse two feet long. They slipped back overboard like pirates and they were all safely back in their boat, rowing past other ships in the harbor, heading up the coast away from the capital, when the dynamite exploded and the vessel went up in flames.

Sitting there in the rowboat, handling an oar, Waters knew he would never forget this, the volume and beauty of the blast, the illumination of the sails by fire, and he watched while the burning vessel tilted and chains and ropes came crashing down. It seemed a ghastly yet magnificent spectacle, and as commotion ensued in the harbor, with bells ringing and sailors shouting, Waters looked back toward the capital, along the coast, to where the American embassy stood, the majestic white building on a cliff by the harbor. From there, in their night apparel, the ambassador and his wife would be able to see the blaze, and Waters would like to have heard them talking about these actions rocking the government. What did they think? Were they aware that their countryman was helping the rebels?

He intended to stay on the island until Garcia payed him his money. To this end, he would drop notes behind at the raids asserting that he would leave the rebels when the General settled his debt. He did wonder how a message could be got to him if Garcia decided to pay, and then there was the question of how could he know that a message from Garcia would not be the lure for an ambush. Somehow something would have to be planned where he could receive the message, slip away from the rebels, get his money, and depart from the island. Impossible? It might be, and he also understood that he would not have an easy time picking up and leaving the rebels. The physical part, vanishing from the rebel camp, he could do, but he was becoming attached to them and had to admit he liked the fighting. Or liked the stimulation that came with the fighting. He felt as alive out on a raid as he did when playing cards, and Waters started telling himself that he'd been fated for this, destined to wind up here. Perhaps this flight from New Orleans and Garcia's welshing on the debt were events that had come to pass in order to lead him to the rebels. They'd happened so he could find a new calling. And what was that calling? What he was doing — fighting, taking up the cause of social justice, wreaking havoc on the aristocrats and their power brokers, the army.

Nonetheless, he had been an aristocrat once, or at least a person descended from privilege. And while he could endure his life with the rebels, sleeping on the ground in the rain, wearing muddy clothes, bathing in rivers, eating fried beans and eggs most nights, every time he thought of his house back home, the mansion with its gables and columns, he would feel familiar pangs. The anguish of loss would weigh on him.

That had been his ancestral home, the place where he had frolicked as a boy, and he'd been raised to appreciate comfort. Despite his maternal lineage, however you cut it, he had lived like an aristocrat. He'd been an upper-class person of fallen stock, without a wife or prospective heirs and without even a crop to grow since he had let his estate grow wild, and the rebels themselves, forgiving him his past, enjoyed hearing him talk about it. They would be there together at night, in the bush, by the fire, passing a bottle of rum around, and he would regale them with the stories of his life gambling for money, living in a house of faded splendor.

"I can't say I didn't love it there. That was my castle."

Conceived during the war, when his father had come home one Easter, he had never seen the estate with cotton or the slaves toiling on it. Sherman's men had burned the fields and the slaves had left at the end of the war. But his mother, the widow, had refused to succumb, and somehow during his childhood years she on her own had kept the house going. She kept them fed and in patched clothes. A Creole of color, a woman who had been pampered as a child and waited on hand and foot as an adult, she had never earned money for herself, but after the war she found a profession teaching French to the children of families still with money in New Orleans. By then she'd hired a cook and maid again and was renting a portion of their land to sharecroppers. Life was improving. But over time she had grown ill, drained and saddened by her years alone, her years of exertion to preserve the house, and with her illness had come debility and long days confined to bed. There in her room with the curtains drawn she would lie in a white or black nightgown, shriveled and weak in its folds, her graying hair loose on the pillows, spread in a fan-shape around her shoulders, and she would travel off in her mind, drifting through memories of his father and the times before the war.

Despite her color, his mother had been the real aristocrat, brought low by history. And she stressed that he would have to marry so he could continue their line. But he'd never married, never wanted to marry, and he'd never cared about the demise of the family name. Espousing solitude and the freedom it brought, he had known from an early age that he was not suited to domestic life, and after taking over the estate, he'd asked the sharecroppers to go. He did not want to have to think about them and mire himself in the world of business. He was supporting himself through poker by that time and kept only the cook and maid.

Though few believed him when he told them, his mother had been the person to teach him poker. He had learned from watching her play, sitting by her during the weekly game she attended. She would play with six other Creole ladies on Saturdays, at the house of whoever was hosting, and he had been captivated by poker, observing everything from his mother's side. By the age of nine or ten, he had gained an understanding of the game, and his mother had been astounded to hear him talking about strategy. After hours and hours of watching, when the game for the day was over, he would bring up a hand she'd lost but should have won. Instead of discarding three cards that hand, she should have dumped two. And another time, she should have gone for the king-high straight. Didn't she see how that person slouched forward whenever he was bluffing? Waters would offer suggestions for future reference, and far from being put off by this, or scared by him, his mother regarded him as blessed, a genius. She taught him what she herself knew about poker. For years afterward, she looked to him for poker advice, and when he was fifteen and she on her deathbed, she told him he had her approval to make his living playing cards. God had given him a talent for gambling, she said, and he would be remiss not to use it.

"You'll have winning days, you'll have losing days. But always keep your temper. There's a game the next night."

Concerning the ups and downs, he had lived up to her exhortation, and never let anger overtake his judgment. When losses happened, as they had to, he would take time to regroup. He'd replay games in his head, identify his blunders. He'd purge his mind of any clutter and gird it for the game to come. It was only in the face of the other stuff, cheating and welshing, that he couldn't keep his equanimity. Over the years, he'd punched people who owed him money, and outside a New Orleans tavern once, right in the street, he'd pistol-whipped a Texan who'd dared do a slight of hand maneuver during a game the night before. The Texan was tall and rangy, with a white beard and long white hair, and Waters accosted him in the tavern.

"Outside," the bartender said. "Now!"

The clientele watched, hushed and expectant, as Waters and the Texan took their bad blood to the street. The Texan's arm moved, but Waters saw it, backhanding the man's gun free after he had pulled it out.

"I want to talk," Waters said. "Do we need guns?"

He kicked the man's pistol away, and while people gathered, at the windows, along the lane, he used his own revolver to beat the Texan bloody.

"I can use my gun, too," he said, when the man fell down. He put his foot on the man's neck, grinding his face into the dirt.

Dishonored, the Texan left New Orleans. The sheriff filed no charges against Waters; players from the game at issue corroborated that the man had cheated. *You cannot let that go*, Waters had thought. *Dishonesty at cards. You have to retaliate.* He didn't know what his mother would think of him for this, or what she would say about the killings he'd done over cards, but he couldn't let himself stew over that. If he'd evolved from a person who punched welshers and cheaters to one who did away with them, so it went. As time passed, everyone changed. And with each killing, he'd acted from the correct position. If poker was your life, as it had been with him, you needed to take the right action to defend it.

Here, living with the rebels, he missed poker. He missed the pleasures unique to poker and thought about them between raids, when he and the others were doing nothing. Then the rebels would start their own games, sitting on their bedrolls during the night, five or six or seven to a group, and Waters would be asked to join in. Everyone was eager to challenge him, and Waters, not wanting to be snobbish, would play. But with the stakes in the games so low, he could not put his heart into it. He knew he was playing with amateurs and didn't like taking their pennies. His wins made him feel like a card sharp exploiting them. But what if he could disguise himself, leave the rebels for a night, and ride down to the capital? He could go play in the casinos. Was that too dangerous? He was so desperate for real poker, against real competitors, for real money, he decided he would have to chance it. But first he put the matter to Amoros, promising that the money he won he would deposit in the rebels coffers.

"I do have a need to play," he said. "Serious poker."

"You might lose."

"I don't think I will."

"You lose sometimes."

"Not when I play on a regular basis."

"Now you want to go often. Can't you live without playing cards?"

They were out of the bush, in the village cantina where they'd first met, sitting at a table drinking rum by themselves. Six others of The Fifty had come to town with them, but three had gone to visit their wives and three to the shack-brothel next door. Waters was thinking of going over also to spend an hour with Rosa, a cigar-smoking woman with raven-black hair, but before he went and asked for her, he hoped he could clarify with Amoros whether or not the rebels would object to his wish to play poker in the capital.

Amoros said they would and that he had no savings anymore. He had given it all to the rebels on joining them. So for him to play cards in the casinos, assuming he could do it without being recognized, he would have to use rebel funds. Money they needed to buy arms, to pay arms smugglers, might be squandered at the tables, all because of his itch to gamble. This could not be allowed, Amoros said, it had to be seen as unacceptable, and the very fact that he wanted to do this called into question his commitment to The Fifty.

"Now you're on Iturbide's side? You don't trust me?"

"I trust you as much as I can," Amoros said.

"But I'm loyal. I've shown that through my fighting."

"You *can* fight," Amoros agreed. "That's true."

"So? Let me play and I'll get you more money for weapons."

The bar was smoky and had a crowd, men in overalls, men in straw hats, women in plain sleeveless frocks. Over near the door, someone was strumming on a guitar. The man played his tune despite laughter and talking and the clinking of the domino pieces, and Waters concentrated on listening. He picked up his glass and drank his rum. In the past, though welcome, Waters had attracted queries and looks when he came into the bar, people asking him what he was up to, whether he'd come on a hunting trip, but no one tonight asked him anything. Everyone knew of his fighting with the rebels and how well he was acquitting himself. It seemed that he'd won most everyone's acceptance, though he was a gringo and came from wealth, and he scolded himself for pestering Amoros with his demands to play high-stakes poker. By all rights, he ought to be thankful the people here had accepted him, and of what importance were his personal needs when there was a rebellion going on and he was an integral part of it?

He rose from the table.

"Think I'll go next door."

"The whorehouse, huh?"

"The whorehouse," Waters said. "I *know* that's not off-limits."

"No," said Amoros. "But is that how you want to spend your night?"

"Can't see why not. I have a little money. I have my take from the last raid."

And Amoros said it was his to spend, but he had something else they could do. He wanted to take Waters on a ride.

"Where?"

"Come with me."

Amoros stood and threw a coin on the table. He let go of another as they left, flipping it at the guitar-strumming man. Outside cicadas were chirping and the smell of cigar smoke, a dense miasma, gave way to the redolent odor of the bush. With the threat of rain building, the air was dank and the sky black as pitch, and the huts in the village lay swathed in a darkness broken only by the candlelight showing in the cracks underneath front doors. Waters could hear the noise from the bar and giggling coming from the whorehouse, but everywhere else in the village it was quiet, wives and men sleeping.

Amoros, by the hitching post, had mounted his horse. Waters untethered his.

"Where we going?" Waters asked again.

"I want to surprise you."

"You're ruining my plans."

"For the whorehouse? You can come into town for that anytime."

So Waters shrugged and got onto his horse and they walked their horses through the village. Then Iturbide appeared in front of them, trotting from the bush on his own mare. Though plump and bowlegged, he could ride well, and Waters knew from having seen him on raids that he was not lacking for fighting skills himself.

He had a gun in his waist holster right now.

"Liquor or a woman?" Waters asked.

"Both," said Iturbide. "Why?"

"Just askin'."

"There's your answer."

Which closed the conversation, and as they passed each other on their horses, Waters saw the loathing in his eyes, the unconcealed hatred in his black face. Would it help if he told Iturbide that he had a Creole mother? Would the man accept him if he said that despite the lightness of his skin he was, in essence, half-black? Waters thought that a one-to-one talk with Iturbide, over drinks, might serve a useful end, and he told Iturbide that he'd be seeing him.

Amoros spoke when they were by themselves again.

"We have to keep you two apart."

"That's not easy."

"I never said it was."

"I should talk to him alone."

"You won't win him over."

"I can try."

Waters mulled over revealing his ancestry to Amoros, but the time didn't seem right for it and he kept his own counsel.

With a kick of his legs and a tug on the reins, Amoros spurred his horse to run. Waters let his piebald follow as they made their exit from the village and entered the greater darkness of the bush. Coming into town from their camp, someone in their group had carried a lantern, and Waters feared they would need one now. He could see nothing. Yet Amoros seemed unbothered by the dark, and not for the first time Waters was amazed at how the rebel leader could ride. Amoros had the eyes of a cat. The bush was as black as it could be, obstructed by low-hanging vines and branches, but Amoros kept leading them along. He called out when to duck and when to turn, when to slow or make his horse leap. It seemed uncanny. But Waters knew there was no mystery here; the rebel's detailed knowledge of the bush came from his years living in it, having to hide and survive in it.

They were up in the highlands, riding across an open ridge, when a misty drizzle began. Silent bursts of lightning came with it and intermittent groans of thunder. Down his spine and along his arms Waters could feel the static in the air, the electrical charge that made his hairs tingle, and he told Amoros that he wanted to get off the ridge. He had known a man hit by lightning in Louisiana, and why should they endanger themselves? But Amoros waved him on, straight as a rail in his saddle, his hair tied back by a red ribbon, and the wildness of the scene, with them on the ridge above the forest, exposed to the lightning, hearing the thunder, summoned for Waters a vision of himself riding toward something momentous. Amoros, dressed in black, looked like an angel of death, and Waters saw himself being led toward a fatal destination. Why Amoros might want to kill him, he didn't know, but the thought made Waters' flesh rise and he felt for the rifle strapped to his horse.

The force of the rain increased, the mist thickened, the flashes of lightning became more frequent. But with all this came a gaseous smell, growing stronger and stronger. Then Amoros veered off the ridge and led him down a rocky slope ending in a narrow ravine, and directly ahead of them Waters saw the white-shrouded entrance to a cave.

"We'll tie up here."

Though on his guard, Waters dismounted. He roped his horse to a stump of wood. He noticed there were numerous streams, crisscrossing trickles with stone beds, and that each stream had a different color, bluish or white or a coppery orange.

"It's the sulfur," Amoros said. "Hot springs."

And Waters then knew the source of the smell billowing out from the holes in the ground and the smoking mouth of the cave, but why had Amoros brought him here? If he meant to kill him, he could have spared them both this ride and had his men do it back in the village.

Waters followed him through the smoke and into the cave's dark mouth. Like himself, Amoros had left his rifle on his horse.

Amoros told him to hold his breath and they went down a passage reeking of sulfur.

"What the hell…"

"Odd, I know," Amoros said.

In the midst of the cave formations, they were back in the open air, though shielded from the rain by a rock overhang. Amoros said he could stop. The rebel leader bent and struck a match and down on the ground an oil lamp flared. Next to it was a rippling pool.

"It's hot but not scalding," Amoros said. "And there's a freshwater spring nearby to cool off."

"But what is this place?"

"My retreat. The place I come to get away."

Amoros had unclasped his belt and was pulling off his riding boots.

"Your retreat?" Waters said. "Is that all? I thought you had something else on your mind."

"Like what?"

"Trying to shoot me."

"Why?"

"I'm not sure. Something to do with my poker request."

But at that Amoros stopped undressing and stared at him with a pained face, and Waters knew he had spoken unfairly. In all his time spent with the fighter he had never seen him look so aggrieved.

"I brought you here so you can see this spot. My sanctuary. I come so I can restore myself and get the peace and quiet to think."

"About what?"

"Battle plans."

By the light from the lamp they both took off their clothes, and Waters was able to confirm something he had suspected about the rebel leader; his body, like his face, was unscarred. For seventeen years and countless raids he had been fighting military governments, living rough in the highlands, and yet no bullet had ever nicked him, no knife had brushed his shadow-thin frame. He was Amoros the Untouchable, and it made Waters see why people had invented legends about him, stories saying he would never be hurt. The stories said he would have to win sometime, lead the rebel forces to victory. How could a man beyond the reach of harm be held down forever?

Amoros was in the hot pool, watching as Waters finished undressing.

"Doesn't this beat going to a whorehouse?"

"I haven't been with a woman in weeks."

"And? Is that so bad?"

Waters said that he'd never been a ladies' man, not with his life devoted to poker and his free hours to riding and hunting, but when he felt his blood heating up he would go and visit a brothel. New Orleans had the best in the world, you know.

"So I've heard," Amoros said.

119

Waters had gotten into the pool, the warmth of it playing over his chest, and he looked up at the rock overhang protecting them from the rain. The downpour was slackening off and the thunder and lightning had become sporadic.

"When we're done," Amoros said, up to his chin in the water, "I'll give you a massage. I learned from a doctor who fought with us once. Killed later — a man I miss. But I have a jar of oil over there and there's nothing like a firm massage for the muscles."

ISOBEL GETS INVOLVED

After a night with a lover, a young man who was the son of the island's French consul, Isobel Paulsen was walking back to the American Embassy residence. She was no stranger to this time of day, the predawn hour, when light from the sun below the horizon turned the far edge of the sea pink, and she glided along in no great rush, enjoying the quiet in the street and the coolness. Before long the cocks would be crowing and the capital awake, with the people and horses in the dirt streets kicking up dust and shaking off flies. The heat would rise as the sun rose, and the day would become bright as flame. Isobel could bear the heat, accustomed as she was to it after ten years of living in the tropics, but these intervals when no one was about and the air not yet scorching always came to her as a tonic. It was something she would look forward to after a nighttime tryst, before she started her walk or ride home. She loved the freshness of the morning in the tropics, and today, she thought, was no disappointment. A warm, salty wind was blowing off the harbor, caressing her body.

To bask in the breeze, she stopped altogether, closing her eyes and gulping in air. She let her head roll around on her shoulders. But then she laughed and kept on going, knowing what was awaiting her at the embassy residence. Sanford would be up, drinking his first glass of rum, and she would sit down to breakfast with him. Over the bread and fruit and coffee he would adopt the hangdog look that expressed his hurt over her amours. How tedious it would all be, how predictable, and she would have to tell him to stop it, remind him again that she loved him despite his drinking and what anybody said. Unlike on Martinique, where the French ruled, her husband was the butt of coarse jokes here because she had a stable of lovers, but if he'd lived with quips for this long, he could go on doing so. Marriage and pleasure were two distinct things for Isobel, and she was unwilling to forgo pleasure in any country.

The street she was on sloped slightly upwards. It ran parallel to the harbor line, far below her at the base of the cliff. As she neared the slope's crest, and the embassy residence, she saw something unexpected, a woman lurching side to side, unsteady on her feet. The woman was in a scarlet cape, and all Isobel could see from behind her was luxuriant black hair. She was inching along the street in the cape, head bowed and arms hidden, the cape's fringe dragging on the hard packed dirt.

Using her Spanish, Isobel spoke to her.

"Señora, can I help you?"

She received no answer and moved closer, still ready to offer assistance. It was then she saw that the object of her attention was in point of fact a girl, twelve or thirteen, pretty. The girl had unblemished light brown skin and eyes shot through with gold, but from the gray cast of her skin, Isobel could see that something was wrong. The grayness was a paleness, a fading of color from her skin. And when Isobel asked again whether she might be of help to the girl, the girl without speaking spread the red cape and presented hands smeared with blood. She was in a spangled gown also drenched with blood, and much of it, to Isobel's horror, looked to be coming from her abdomen.

"What happened?" said Isobel, but the girl furnished no information. She hung her head, eyes down. In addition to her pain, the girl was frightened, and Isobel reasoned that she had to be disoriented. Even as she stood with her cape wide open and the grisly bloodstains showing, she seemed distant. Her lips were parted, her eyelids fluttering. Then her legs gave out and she sagged towards the ground, but Isobel managed to break her fall by jumping forward with her arms outstretched. She saw that the girl had fainted; her eyes were shut and she lay insensible. Faced with the choice of running to get help or trying to lug her up the hill, Isobel chose to move her herself when she felt how light the girl was — like a pillow stuffed with feathers — and in her arms she hauled her up the street all the way to the embassy residence.

Her husband was awake in his pajamas, reading in his bed under the mosquito net. Consistent to form, he had a glass of rum in his hand and gave Isobel a sorrowful look as soon as she entered the room. But the worry on her face must have told him this was not the time for theatrics, his routine of self-pity, and after taking a sip of his rum, he asked her what was wrong. She answered, telling him about the girl she'd found, and she said that a doctor should be summoned because the girl might bleed to death.

"My God! How old is she?"

"I don't know yet," Isobel said. "She's too scared to talk."

Isobel had rung for the housekeeper and left the girl with her in the parlor. As she returned there now, she brought her husband's bottle of rum, thinking it might revive the girl. But the housekeeper, a Martinican woman who had come with them from that island, was one step ahead of her; she'd taken the brandy from the cabinet. She'd filled a glass and carried it back to the sofa, and while Isobel cradled the girl's head, she tipped the brandy down her throat.

"But this is horrible. Did someone do that to her?"

Isobel turned and saw her husband. He was in the doorway. He had draped a green robe over his pajamas and from the glassiness in his eyes, she thought he might faint himself. Blood was a sight he could not stand, and since the girl's cape was lying open, the blood on her was visible.

"I don't know," Isobel said. "But she needs a doctor."

"I can see that," Sanford said.

"Should I go myself or will you send for him?"

Her husband went and Isobel endured the tense moments of waiting. What could explain why the girl had been out in the street so early, wandering around in a daze? There was too much blood for her to be bleeding from natural causes relating to womanhood, and she did look as she lay on the sofa, restored to consciousness by the brandy, like a person who had been hurt, not just shaken by a bodily function. Despite the ministrations of the housekeeper, who dabbed at her face with a cloth, the girl moaned and clutched at her abdomen, and when Isobel inquired again, asking in her tenderest voice what had happened, she bit her lip and shook her head as if she could not dare speak of her misfortune.

The doctor came and went to work. Isobel had transferred the girl to a guest bedroom, and to leave the doctor by himself, she and her husband withdrew to the parlor. They drank the coffee the housekeeper poured them. After more waiting, the doctor joined them, wizened face somber as a death mask, and though he said the girl would live, he reported that she had been violated. It was unspeakable. The damage done would probably heal and he had succeeded in stopping the blood flow, but the girl would say nothing of what had transpired or anything about her family.

"She could be an orphan," the doctor said. "That's my guess."

"I'll try to find out," Isobel answered.

"And she'll have to have rest for a while," he said. "Someone to look after her."

"I'll do it."

The doctor said that might be best until the girl recovered, and he told Isobel he would come back later, early that night, to see how she was getting on.

"I gave her something to sleep," he said. "It should last the day."

Black case in hand, he took himself off. Isobel called to the housekeeper and said that their breakfast could be served. She felt glad she had rescued the girl, but before she could relax inside, her husband voiced reservations he had to keeping the girl in the house with them. Caring for the ailing was not their province and he did not want to set a precedent. Supposed all the island's sick came shuffling to their door? They ran an embassy, not a clinic, and they should remember that.

"You would have me throw her back out?" said Isobel.

"She's not our responsibility."

"What is here?" Isobel asked. "To sit around and do nothing?"

"There's the hospital in town."

"You call that a hospital? This girl has been horribly hurt by someone and I'm not going to put her out till she's better. I can't believe you."

Her husband's indifference nauseated her and she told him he should forget about the girl by doing what he normally did — passing his day in a drunken stupor.

The girl slept through the morning and afternoon. Isobel looked in on her repeatedly, noting the color returning to her skin. She slept the entire time on her back, in a white nightdress Isobel had provided, and though she cried out on occasion, as if having bad dreams, her sleep on the whole appeared restful.

It was getting toward dusk, the hour of the fireflies, when Isobel entered the room again and saw the girl awake in the bed, gazing at her from under the mosquito net. She tried to make the girl feel welcome by sitting on the bed and introducing herself, and she assured the girl that she was safe here, in the care of people who wanted to help her.

The girl spoke.

"I'm hungry, señora."

"You can have food."

"And señora? I'm thirsty."

"We'll fix something up for you right now."

The girl uttered her thanks and averted her eyes to the floor. She had articulated her words timidly, from behind a veil of black hair, and her shyness moved Isobel. Convinced by her manner that she was a peasant girl unaccustomed to compassion, she meant to find out the specifics of her story. But she decided she would save the questions for later, when the girl hopefully would be more at ease, and concentrated for the time being on hurrying off to the kitchen to get something prepared for her. She viewed her desire for food as an indication of improving spirits and expected the doctor to be pleased by her progress when he arrived later in the evening.

The doctor did not come, however. Nor did he send Isobel a message. As the hours passed and the sky got dark, Isobel became perturbed by this, and she had a servant go to his house to bring him over without delay.

The servant, returning, walked into the parlor with her head down. She was the housekeeper's assistant, a girl from the island who spoke better Spanish than the Martinican woman, and Isobel rose from the sofa to ask her why the doctor had not come with her. Was something preventing him from coming? The girl nodded but said nothing, looking away toward the wall, and this gust of evasiveness reminded Isobel of the girl in the bedroom. The housekeeper's assistant knew Isobel, but was no less circumspect, frightened by something she had learned, and presently she took a string from her frock and weaved it around her calloused fingers. In the multi-colored frock and her blue kerchief she stood before Isobel staring at the floor, shifting from foot to foot, and all she would say in response to questions was that the doctor refused to come. Incredulous, Isobel asked whether he had given her an explanation. The girl said no. The doctor's attendant had met her at the door and conveyed the news from his master, and then the door had been shut in her face. But she did add, as Isobel gaped, that the man had opened the door again and whispered something else to her; he'd told her to tell the ambassador's wife that the doctor's spurning of his duties had a connection to General Garcia. That afternoon, the man went on, two emissaries from the General had payed the doctor a visit, and it seemed they had ordered him not to see the girl taken in by Mrs. Paulsen.

Isobel was stunned. "What does the General have to do with it?"

"Señora, can I go now?"

"How does he know the girl is here?"

"Nothing much is secret on this island, señora."

Isobel could vouch for that. News of every stripe spread through servants and the like. But she was mystified by this turn of events and found herself confronting again the need to question the girl in the bedroom.

She went about this delicately, waiting until the next morning when the girl joined her for breakfast in the dining room. In actuality, Isobel had eaten, but she invited the girl to the table so they could develop a rapport. She wanted the girl to feel calm in her presence and know that she could confide in her. Sanford had removed himself from the dining room, plodding off to his study to do his correspondence, and when the girl sat down in the muslin robe Isobel was letting her wear, the housekeeper padded in with a tray. She had milk and tea and biscuits and butter as well as a dish of peeled oranges.

The housekeeper (her name was Francine) had told Isobel the previous night that she could do the doctor's job. Whatever the doctor might prescribe for the girl, she could administer herself, though her medicines would be herbal ones, remedies of her own creation. She'd told Isobel she would start in the morning by putting something in the girl's tea, something to dull the physical pain the girl must be feeling inside, and Isobel had given her assent. She'd watched Francine use her healing powers both on this island and Martinique, and trusted the woman's medicinal knowledge.

Allowed to rest and to eat her fill, the girl over the next day or two did begin to come out of her shell. Isobel's kindness and Francine's powders had a beneficial effect. The combination wore down her timidity, and that first evening, while Isobel was playing her piano with the windows onto the veranda open, she appeared in the room's doorway as if she wanted to enter and listen. Scott Joplin had pulled her from bed. From her wonderstruck face one would have thought she had never heard a piano before, and Isobel waved her into the room saying she should sit on the chaise lounge. She knew that with time the girl would talk, answer questions, say something about herself; and the time came that very night after the girl had got into bed. Francine served her a bowl of hot milk. Isobel was tucking her in when the girl said something about going home to see her parents and her brothers.

"You have a mother and father?" asked Isobel.

"Yes, señora."

"How old are you?"

"Thirteen."

"And where are your parents?"

"At home. In our village."

"Your village. What took you away from there?"

The girl recoiled, biting her lip, and the glimmer of tears could be seen in her eyes, about to spill over onto her cheeks.

"It was the General, señora."

"General Garcia?"

She moved her head up and down.

"What exactly did he do to you?"

Isobel could imagine what, but she wanted no misunderstandings. She needed to hear it from the girl's lips. And that was when the girl told her, describing as the tears burst forth how armed soldiers had come to her house, spoken with her parents, put her on a horse, and conducted her to the General's palace. There she had been washed and fed and dressed in the spangled gown, all so the naked general, in a room painted red, could do what he'd done to her. Before he got to finish, though, she had begun to bleed like mad and the General had turned red with rage. He'd gone berserk, screaming at her, threatening to feed her to the dogs outside, and after that another man had walked in and thrown the gown and cape over her. In terror, she'd begged for her life, and the man had whisked her out of the palace to leave her somewhere in the street.

"That's how you found me, señora. I was walking, I think, and you found me."

An inkling of what the General practiced crossed Isobel's mind. She felt disgust rising in her, an icy fury. But she knew that she had no legitimate power over what the General did, and she also had to contend with Sanford since he was still complaining about the girl being in their house. For the last two days he'd done nothing but avoid the girl, not once asking after her condition. And that night, in his bedroom, after Isobel had done what she could to comfort the girl, staying by her side till she fell asleep, promising that she would see her parents soon, he was repellent. He threw up his hands and rolled over in his bed when Isobel repeated the girl's story.

"So he likes women young," Sanford said, talking in the direction of the wall. "Not admirable, but that's his prerogative."

"Young? The girl's a child."

"I'm sorry she got hurt."

"And you don't object that he uses soldiers to procure them."

"It's his personal business. Not ours."

"But propping up the man is."

"His troops are demoralized and the government's crumbling," Sanford said. "I think that's what's relevant now."

With respect to the status of the army, Sanford was not exaggerating. The rebel forces had not been defeated anywhere in weeks. They'd overrun three military depots, seizing all weapons and ammunition, and had raided and sacked enough country mansions to terrify most landowners. Their estates left in the hands of overseers, or scorched by fires the rebels had set, these aristocrats fled for safety to their houses in the capital. They feared they were losing a grip on the country. The rebels controlled the bush and the highlands to a greater extent than ever, and with the army proving ineffective, there were calls coming from the rich for the Americans to intervene. They should send in their troops and rout the rebels as they'd done during other bad times.

General Garcia resisted, however. He did not want American help, or "interference" as he phrased it. He kept averring that he had the country firmly in hand and that all American nationals and American companies operating on the island were secure. He told Ambassador Paulsen that the sugar, pineapple and banana plantations owned by American interests were under extra tight military guard and that none, furthermore, had been attacked. No American-held property had been touched. This was a clue that the rebels were afraid to engage his men in direct combat and had to resort to their lowdown tactics of scratching here and pricking there, like gnats.

In a letter to Paulsen written in Spanish and sent through an underling, he said that his men would rebound and were formulating a new counterattack strategy.

"Tell your friends in Washington not to get worked up," he wrote. "And tell the Marines to keep their asses away from here, too."

When Isobel saw this message, she gave out a snort, tickled by the General's bravado, as unimpressed with a man as she could be. But then she had never liked General Hernandez Garcia Napoles, with his fat cigars and pasty cheeks and that bubble of a belly, and after this incident with the young girl she felt him deserving of castration. So when Sanford told her, with a wrinkled-stressed face, that he had scheduled to meet with Garcia to discuss his note and the conflict in general, Isobel said she was coming also. She intended to say her piece in the palace conversation.

"This won't be about his personal habits," Sanford said.

"I'm aware of that."

"It's official ambassador's business."

"Don't get so stuffy, Sanford."

"But why don't you see him tomorrow? By yourself."

"I'm coming with you," she said. "I want to hear what he has to say."

The meeting took place in the General's office. Garcia, in full regalia — a green uniform, peaked cap, and black boots — was seated at his desk, and two of his officers were sitting in the old mahogany chairs the Spanish governor had once owned. They too were wearing their uniforms, blue-green, with rank-denoting bars on the breast, and neither one offered his chair to Ambassador Paulsen. When he entered the room, they nodded at him with curt formality. But the thin-lipped one, Colonel Bosch, rustling with the starch in his uniform, shot to his feet and made a stiff bow when Isobel came in behind him. Sanford explained that his wife wanted to join in their talk, add her ideas, and despite the apologetic tones he used, Colonel Bosch clasped her hand and bent over from the waist to kiss it. This gallantry, which she found unctuous, amused Isobel, but she could sense that Garcia's men were relieved she'd come. It was no secret that her husband, with his laziness and drinking, commanded little respect from the military, while she, known for her clarity of mind, did. Whatever advice they could swallow their pride to solicit, they would seek from her, not him, and it wouldn't be the first time they had done this.

For all that, Isobel kept silent during their talk. She accepted the chair Bosch had vacated and asked her to take, and then sat with her hands in her lap and an eye on Garcia. She knew that he knew that she still had the injured girl at her house, and Isobel was wondering whether this might cause him anxiety. No idiot, Garcia had to know that she deplored what he was doing to young girls. All presidents on the island, like it or not, were obliged to consider how their American backers perceived them, and she wanted Garcia to understand that she could turn her distaste for him into something more consequential, a problem in his relations with Washington. She wanted him not to forget that he was in power because he was useful to the United States of America, and somebody else, Colonel Bosch for instance, could rapidly be hoisted to president if she or her husband pulled strings. The island supported American business interests and was important for the protection of sea routes to the canal the United States was building in Panama. Much less important was the person running the government.

If any of this was swirling in his thoughts, Garcia Napoles did not show it. Erect in the chair behind his desk, hands folded on his green paper blotter, the General maintained a detached expression while Bosch summarized for the Paulsens' benefit the present military situation. The other officer there, dark as a coffee bean, with curly hair under his cap, expounded on points Bosch had neglected, and the overall picture Isobel drew, hard as they tried to understate it, was that the army did need help. In the wake of their recent losses, the army had control of the capital and the southern lowland areas — the casinos were in the capital, the American-owned fruit plantations in the south — but how long could the country survive divided, with the rebels dominating the bush and the highlands? Unless an offensive was undertaken, and the rebels once and for all were crushed, the current regime could be toppled. At best, if there was no change in the situation, they could expect a standoff with the rebels, a long war of attrition, and the stature of the rebel leader, Raoul Amoros, would grow and grow and grow.

"The man's already a legend," Sanford said. "Admit that. It's imperative that he, he above everyone else, be killed."

"Cut off the snake's head and the body dies," Colonel Bosch said.

But the General remained ostentatiously aloof. He selected a cigar from a box on his desk, snipped the end with scissors, lit a match, and sat back in his cushioned seat to smoke. "A Havana," he said, admiring it, holding it out for all to see, and then he took an extended puff and let out the smoke in a series of circles. The cigar's smell permeated the office, and even with the plushy green and gold curtains drawn across the window to block out the sun, the room was a broiling oven. Everybody there was sweating. To Isobel the men's uniforms were inappropriate — close-fitting and buttoned to the neck — and her husband too, in his beige suit and tie, looked as if he felt constricted, daubing his forehead every few minutes with a white monogrammed handkerchief. She herself had on a white dress, modest in how it was cut and shaped but cool as a dress could be in this weather, and with her hair pinned up and a fan in her hand she felt she could withstand the heat.

There had been a lull in the conversation, each of them waiting for the General to speak. But he kept puffing on his cigar, blowing the smoke out in rings. Isobel fanned herself in her chair, the officer in the other chair crossed and uncrossed his muscular legs, and over by the brocade curtains Sanford stood picking at his handkerchief. Jerky in his movements, wetting his lips with his tongue, the ambassador looked like he wanted a drink, but pride would not allow him to ask for one. He stood mum despite his need, and Bosch alone, pacing the floor boards, made any appreciable noises. Now and again the colonel would clear his throat, and he did this so emphatically Isobel thought he was sending a message. He seemed to be saying their talk was not over and decisions had to be reached soon.

Isobel ended the silence herself.

"What about Jack Waters?"

Colonel Bosch halted and the curly-haired officer flinched in his chair. The two of them fixed their eyes on her and Isobel felt she must have said something deemed impolitic. Was it the name itself? Jack Waters?

In palace circles and among the rich he had become a notorious person, the American seen riding with the rebels and helping them destroy haciendas, but in her role as the wife of the US ambassador, she thought it her duty to concern herself with him. An enemy or not, he was an American citizen, and she had a theory about the man at odds with prevailing notions.

"We have a rule here," the colonel said. "No one but the General mentions his name."

"Jack Waters?"

"Yes," said the colonel.

"Why?"

"General's orders. Unless he mentions Waters, nobody talks about him."

This injunction sounded asinine, but there was no mistaking the colonel's earnestness. And Isobel noticed that Garcia had snapped upright in his chair. He had his cigar clamped between his teeth, and through the wisps of smoke in the room, she saw his lumpy face reddening. Gone in a second was the disinterest he had been flaunting, and Isobel, though she'd done it by accident, rejoiced at having scraped a nerve.

"There's nothing to say about the man," said the General. "He's fighting with the rebels and will be hunted down and killed like all the others. Like a dog."

"And you're sure he believes in their cause?" Isobel asked.

"What a question! How can he not?"

"He may well not."

"He's fighting with them, isn't he?"

"But *why* is he? *Why* is he out with them is the question?"

Isobel knew she had to expand on what she meant, and she took time to figure out how. As she did, she looked over at her husband, still standing by the curtains, but she knew she would get no help from him. What she was about to put to Garcia, she and Sanford had discussed between themselves, but God forbid that Sanford raise the topic with the General himself! Sanford returned the look she gave him with a squint that urged clamming up, and she felt that both Colonel Bosch and the other officer were holding their breath for her, tense with a fear that Garcia Napoles would call palace guards and have her hung if she pushed this line of enquiry. For heaven's sake! Did nobody ever stand up to the General?

Isobel said that her husband had delved into Jack Waters' past. To establish that he was from New Orleans, as he claimed, Sanford had cabled the authorities there, supplying a description of Jack Waters, asking if they had any record of the man. And they had cabled back, telling him of an arrest warrant out for a man of that name and description; he was a fugitive from the law for a murder committed five months ago. Another cable from Sanford had asked for a letter of explication, and two weeks later this missive had arrived with facts about Waters, and his history. It seemed that during a poker game on the country estate he owned a man had been caught with cards up his sleeve. An irate Waters, despite four witnesses, had leaped across the poker table and knifed the man in the heart. Since no one there had tried to detain him, Waters had been able to flee, and he had never been heard from again. A reward for his capture, dead or alive, had been posted by the victim's father, but the sheriff of the parish where Waters lived had all but given up hope of ever finding him. The witnesses pleaded ignorance when asked where he'd gone, and the sheriff's threats to charge them with aiding and abetting a fugitive had elicited nothing either. In the sheriff's opinion, they honestly did not know where

Waters had run to, and he'd told his deputy the case was at a dead end.

Isobel stopped. The men didn't speak. She felt herself breathing fast and her throat was dry from all the smoke in the room.

"Doesn't this sound familiar?" she asked.

Still nobody else spoke, though she heard a moan come from her husband. The General looked at his cigar stub.

"This is a man," Isobel said, "who has no political history. He's done no political fighting anywhere. What he doesn't like are people who cheat at cards."

"Nobody's cheated him," Colonel Bosch said.

"Welshing qualifies," Isobel said. "Not paying up on debts."

The General grinned, red-faced in his chair, and Isobel smiled right back at him.

"You gringos," the General said. "You always stick together."

Isobel said she was not excusing Waters' actions, only trying to comprehend them, and she restated her belief that Waters' aid to the rebel cause had nothing to do with politics. It was rooted in a personal grievance, the General's refusal to pay him the money he had won in their poker game.

"I didn't pay him because of the rebels. Everything he won would go to the rebels."

"Who says?"

"Everybody."

"That's what they said. But nobody has proof to support it."

The General sneered and tossed his head, but Colonel Bosch took up her argument. He intimated that she might be correct. He informed her of the notes Waters had left at his raid sites, scribbled notes in which he said he would leave the rebels and the island if and when he got his money. Doubtless, this could be a ruse on Waters' part to bilk the General of that money so as to buy the rebels more arms, but if Waters was sincere, then they might have a chance to negotiate with him. After what he'd done, they would never just pay him and grant him an amnesty, but why could they not try to entice him into divulging rebel plans? If he was as mercenary as the Señora painted him, they might be able to buy his services for a price above the price of the debt.

"He could be our man," Bosch said. "This would be how we catch Amoros."

But the General refused to discuss it. "No," he said, and again: "No." The cigar stump between his teeth, he trained his stony eyes on Bosch and ran one hand over his chin. Then he thanked everyone for coming to the meeting and swore that the army would wipe out the rebels, but Colonel Bosch, his mettle up, would not be dismissed so easily. The colonel demanded that his plan for Waters be accorded due consideration, and as though all fear had gone from him he said this with aggressive defiance. Isobel was no fonder of him than she was of the General — he was a prudish man who had criticized her for taking lovers, contending that she would go to hell for adultery — but she winked at him for taking a stand. For now, in this office, she saw him as her ally. And by making no move to rise from her chair, she too let the General know she would not be going yet.

"General Garcia, he's an American, and you treated him unjustly," she said.

"He's a criminal," Garcia replied. "And if I were you, I'd be careful in what I say."

Sanford now re-entered the talk, stepping away from the shadow by the curtains. In what he called a stroke of inspiration, he suggested that they print a one-page notice pledging a pardon and a settling of the debt if Waters came out of the bush. The chances were slim he would accept this, as he would be looking for a trap, but in the event that he did, they would have him in their custody. They could do what they wanted with him then, but if his allegiance to the rebels was phony, as Isobel said, they might be able to cut a deal with him and buy information on the rebels from him. Conversely, if he did not respond to the notice, as was likely, the rebels might do their work for them. The paper might have the effect of creating suspicion among the rebels, casting doubt on his loyalty to them, and who knows, they might kill him themselves. In either scenario, irrespective of Waters' response, the notice could not do harm to the General, and it could be scattered across the island to ensure that the rebels see it.

"What do you think?" Sanford asked in conclusion.

Isobel thought Garcia would laugh, or reject the idea out of stubbornness, but to her consternation he did nothing of the sort. The General embraced the plan. He professed amazement that it was Sanford's, Sanford being useless most often, drunk or asleep at the embassy, but said that they could give it a try. As concocted, it could not but put Jack Waters in a bind. The General said that he wanted the plan carried out straight away, and he put Colonel Bosch in charge.

"Oversee the printing and the distribution of the notice."

"I will, General."

"That is, if the plan appeals to you, Colonel. If you're willing to carry it out for us."

"I am, General."

"Glad to hear it, Colonel Bosch. We wouldn't want to do anything without your consent."

Colonel Bosch, Isobel reflected, had best watch his step with the General. He should not go too far in angering him. Continue this way, and the colonel might drown in his bath one night, or have a fatal riding accident. Yet Bosch seemed to know the General, how to switch tacks when talking to him, and humility came into his voice.

"The gringo's a thief and a dog, General. As you said yourself."

With something of import decided, the meeting disbanded, and although Sanford walked out looking cheerful, delighted with himself for having been of use, Isobel felt a gnawing frustration. The meeting had not gone as she hoped. She had never got to speak about the girl Garcia had violated, and she felt a partiality toward this man named Jack Waters. She liked what he represented, a thorn in the General's mind, and wished him well in his quest to get the money Garcia owed him. Rebel confederate or not, fugitive murderer or not, the man Jack Waters had character and what could be defined as a sense of justice. Unfortunately, the idea hatched by her husband was one that would make his life difficult. She asked herself, "Is there anything I can do to help him?"

THE CAVE

For Isobel, what came next was a worrisome time. She felt powerless. She had half-expected her husband not to follow through on his plan, but two days after their meeting with the General, Sanford, accompanied by Colonel Bosch, went to the island's newspaper publisher and enjoined him to use his printing press to churn out hundreds of copies of the notice Sanford himself had written. That night over dinner he showed her one, and he crinkled his face with the certainty that he had accomplished something useful. Let those who liked to belittle him, or call him worthless for his drinking, remember during the times to come that he'd been the man to step in. As Sanford envisioned it, and explained it, beaming in the dining room's candlelight as he sipped a red imported from France, his note would have to jar the rebels and throw their camp into disruption. Everyone knew, from the whispers all around, that Jack Waters was a hero with the rebels, looked on by them now as a tested compatriot, but if doubt could be cast over his motives, his loyalty to their cause put in question, the morale of the rebels might be hurt and a germ of mistrust unleashed among them.

"It's their tightness that hurts us," Sanford said. "But if we get them suspecting each other, betraying each other…"

Isobel laughed. She told her husband he was losing perspective. She said that his note might well lead to Jack Waters' death, his execution by the rebels, but the course of the fighting would not be changed because the rebels had one less man.

"They've been tight and they'll stay tight," she said. "Tell your generals that."

"Only Garcia has the rank of general."

"General, colonel…Do you take their ranks seriously?"

"I have a job to do," Sanford said. "And I'm trying damn hard to do it."

Isobel allowed him his delusion. Suddenly he wanted to be active instead of lost in an alcohol fog dreaming of Europe. But underneath the talk, if she knew her husband, he still resented being stationed here, on this speck in the ocean as he dubbed it, and she could see him in a week or so reverting to his standard self. There he would be, sallow and drunk, lying shirtless in his hammock, and he would be mumbling to himself about the unimportance of the island. Soon, as in the past, he would be complaining about Garcia and the whims of this "tinhorn despot."

Under Bosch's command, army troops on their horses were to scatter copies of the note tomorrow morning. They would drop them around the capital and throughout the southern lowland areas, and they would leave them in the hills and bush. On no part of the island would a rebel or a rebel sympathizer not happen across a copy, and before he went to bed that night, Sanford predicted that by tomorrow evening Jack Waters would be dead, facing rebel interrogation, or on the run for his life. He didn't think Waters would take the offer in the note and come to the capital for the money the President owed him, but he had written that should Waters do that he should come to the US Embassy. Sanford, in the note, was positioning himself as the mediator in the dispute between Jack Waters and Garcia, and he was saying that as ambassador he could guarantee Waters his safety if Waters emerged from the bush and presented himself at the US embassy.

Isobel went to her room and the night dragged. In her bed, under her mosquito net, she found herself unable to sleep. Jack Waters' plight bothered her more than she'd thought it would, and though she understood that she might be putting the man on a pedestal he neither wanted nor deserved, she gave herself a searing headache pondering ways she could help him. Why should General Garcia, corrupt Garcia, violator of young girls, be permitted to triumph in this? Why should he even be in power anymore? With his army struggling and low in confidence, with his commanders, men like Colonel Bosch, showing irritation with him, maybe the time had come for a change. The pretext could be the General's refusal to accept help from the US military, and the right word from herself or Sanford could convince Washington to dislodge him.

These were Isobel's reflections as the night crept along. Several times she rose, rubbing her temples, going to her window and leaning out, and she didn't feel her headache subside until the sky was brightening. Despite her resolve to have Garcia ousted, she had admitted to herself that she could do nothing for Jack Waters, and as she lay staring through the window, she said a silent prayer for him. She prayed that he would escape somehow, get off the island, this curious man so full of pride who would not brook the slightest injustice done to himself for any reason, and she imagined herself meeting him one day, somewhere else, and congratulating him on his escape. Then she was asleep, or almost, and somewhere that seemed far away she could hear raindrops falling. Outside, in the warm gray dawn, it had begun to drizzle.

Francine awoke her with raps on her door, announcing breakfast. Isobel inhaled the cool moist air and opened her eyes to the sight of the rain falling in sheets past her window. She felt as if she had gotten no rest and might stay in bed till lunch, but then she decided she would get up now, eat something, and return to bed. She could do with food after her long bout of insomnia.

Across the table, in his beige morning robe, Sanford looked glum.

"What's wrong with you?" Isobel asked.

"We had to postpone things. No sending out the note today."

"The rain?"

"What else? The notes will get soaked and ruined."

Perhaps her prayer had worked. The rain continued to pour down throughout the day and night. It did not let up the next day either, and under skies varying from charcoal-black to ash-gray, the island became a drowned mess. Rivers and streams overflowed; the streets in the capital turned to mud; every trail across the island, whether in the hills, lowlands, or bush, was transformed into a bog. The winds were not severe, though — this was not a hurricane — and only trees rotting already, or slender and fragile in their construction, cracked or swayed or fell to the ground. For a rainstorm this heavy, the air was tranquil, with the sea around the island barely stirred up, and Isobel checked a calendar once to verify the time of year. As she had known all along, this was not the rainy season.

Limited to the house, Isobel made the best of her time. She played her piano, working on her ragtime pieces, and read through her journal. For the decade they'd lived abroad, she had been keeping this informal diary, and she was planning to cull it for her novel. Meanwhile, there was a story unfolding here, the story of the girl she had found pale and bleeding in the street. Under the care of herself and Francine, the pretty girl had recovered her strength, and she was eating heartily. The color was back in her light brown skin and she could walk without pain. But whereas before, days ago, she had been longing to head home and see her parents and brothers, now she was resistant to going. She was afraid her family would repudiate her for what had happened at the palace.

"But the general took you against your will."

"I was supposed to come back with money."

"From whom?"

"The general."

"That's what he said?"

"Every girl he picks brings back money. But not if he didn't like them."

Isobel hung her head. She was ignorant of so much happening on this island. But she had herself alone to blame; she spent too much of her time in the embassy and not enough going out and about. She was overly involved with her own pursuits, the piano and her book, and when she did go out, it was for a dinner or an amorous tryst, something centered on pleasure and amusement. Her set was the wealthy, the people on the island who owned estates, ran the casinos, or were diplomats, and for a fleeting but powerful moment she felt revulsion for herself.

"I'll take you home myself," she said. "I'll explain everything. Your family will be overjoyed to see you."

She promised they would go when the rain stopped and told the girl all would be well. But the girl still looked unconvinced and kept to herself in the guest bedroom. The girl was shy by nature, presumably, and she must have heard Sanford asking when she would be gone from the house. He did this at every meal, shouting the question at Isobel, but Isobel would not answer. She let her face express the anger she was feeling over his attitude. In his new guise as busy ambassador trying to help the current regime, Sanford was willing to overlook the general's practices with young girls. He kept calling that "private behavior" not for them to meddle with, and Isobel realized that with this viewpoint Sanford could become her enemy. It would be difficult, if not impossible, to persuade Washington to oust Garcia if her husband was against the removal, and Isobel saw that unless he reverted to his old self, drunk and apathetic, uncaring in the main, he could pose a problem.

She was thinking about this possibility, and how she might respond to it, when the rainstorm finally ceased and the sun reappeared. It was early in the morning, like when the rain had started, and Sanford got dressed and left the house to tell Colonel Bosch to send out his men with the notes about Jack Waters. The deluge had lasted three days and it seemed as if nature, the skies above, had given Waters those days to escape. But in all likelihood he hadn't gone, being unaware of what lay in store for him, and Isobel foresaw him dying. Incensed by the revelations in the note, the rebels would stand him up and shoot him. Then again, she could be wrong and the rebels might not be so draconian, but Isobel Paulsen felt in her bones that Jack Waters, during this rainstorm, had lived the last three days of his life.

For the three days it rained, the rebels suspended all offensive activity. They were as surprised as anyone else that the storm had hit now, out of season, and with their camps in the hills turned to muck, they brought their horses, weapons, and blankets down into the bushland villages. Here, for the length of the downpour, they rested. This was a time to relax with wives and children, eat food cooked in an oven, luxuriate in a heated bath. During the nights the rum flowed and inside the huts there were lantern-lit fiestas. While guitars were played or drums palm-tapped, voices thick with passion or weariness sang songs of love and nostalgia. Old men, who had fought against prior governments, and lost a limb for their efforts, would sit in the corners and bark violent words about the need to continue the fight until the army soldiers were beaten. The cantinas filled, loud with laughter and battle stories, and village brothels saw a rise in business as the rebel fighters migrated to their doors. The break in the fighting was a welcome thing for everyone concerned, and in the huts, at the fiestas, a tentative optimism could be felt. Raoul Cardenes Amoros, leading the rebels for seventeen years, a survivor despite failed revolts in the past, had never before been so close to victory. Everybody knew that the military was licking its wounds and in disarray, and once the rainstorm ended, it was hoped a final push on the capital might be possible. The army, with its morale so low, might collapse. Yet there were those who did raise the specter of the infernal goddamned Yankees, the Marines, and what would happen if they invaded as they had done here before.

Amoros, during the storm, wrestled with this question himself. While his men sought diversion and familial warmth back home in their villages, he stayed behind in the northern highlands and rode his horse to his cave retreat. He took supplies and his bedroll with him and he invited Jack Waters along. He told Waters that he wanted a gringo mind to help him chart his strategy. If he and the Fifty were to take the capital, seize power, what could they do to keep the Yankees away? Could they placate Washington somehow? Waters insisted that he had no insight into the US military, that he could offer no wisdom into the methods of the American government, that political analysis of any kind was a skill beyond his depth, but Amoros said not to worry and asked him regardless to come to the cave. What he needed, he said, was a sounding board for his ideas. And he said all this in a secretive whisper, his mouth against Waters' ear, so as not to let his other men know he would be using Waters as a confidante.

This was before all the men had broken camp and gone back to their villages. They were assuming that Amoros would go off to his cave alone, as he habitually did. He would spend his days strategizing there, and after that he would ride back to camp for open discussions on his plans. He seldom had anyone join him in the cave (he did his best thinking in seclusion, he said), and to tell his men he was bringing Waters there might unsettle them. The majority of the men, by this time, saw Jack Waters as a comrade, but a small group in the Fifty did not. Their leader, Commander Iturbide, still had him pegged as a white southern gringo who might be a spy for the government, and from the men in his group there had come stated opposition over the degree to which Amoros seemed to be confiding in Waters. More agitation, at this crucial juncture, Amoros wanted to avoid, so he told Jack Waters to ride off by himself and then double back through the bush to meet him later at the cave.

To accommodate Amoros, Waters did as he was asked. He led his piebald away from the camp, toward the southern villages, and then around in a circular route back toward the northern highlands. From his earlier visits to the cave-retreat, he knew how to get there in the dark, but the paths in the rain were treacherous. The dirt was sloshy, and the ridge above the cave as slippery as ice. But he made it through the forest and across the ridge and down the slope into the ravine, and at last, dripping wet, he pulled up at the mouth of the cave. He sucked in the heat and white steam rising from the springs nearby. For once, the smell of the sulfur did not put him off, and he found Amoros waiting for him, sitting by a fire inside the cave.

"Get undressed," Amoros said. "Warm yourself with a bath."

Waters took off his clothes and submerged himself in a pool. Afterwards, back in the cave, he submitted himself to an Amoros massage. He lay flat and naked on a mat by the fire, his skin tingling from his bath, and Amoros applied the oil from a jar while running chapped hands over his muscles.

"The body's like a gun," Amoros said. "Care for it, keep the parts oiled, and it won't let you down."

He had his eccentricities, Waters thought, but how could he argue with a man who'd lived through seventeen years of fighting? Seventeen years and not a mark on his body, not a single contusion or scar. Whatever he believed about bodily maintenance, it had been working like magic for him, and on top of everything else he did, Amoros gave exquisite massages. No nurse in a spa, trained in the art, could have done better.

For three days, as the rain fell, Waters and Amoros talked. The fire and an oil lamp gave light, and in their pots they cooked dried pork, bananas, yams, and rice. From the drinkable streams outside they got water, dipping their canteens, and neither required a blanket to sleep since the cave was so warm.

Shirtless, they lounged on their mats while they talked, or they would undress altogether and enjoy themselves in the pools. Waters did more listening than speaking, and at times he would find himself dozing off despite the solemnity in Amoros' voice. He had to keep apologizing. Exhaustion had set in, he realized, after all these weeks of living in the highlands, moving from camp to camp, grabbing catnaps, and sleeping light sleeps interrupted by showers. Though he prided himself on his ruggedness, he yearned for a leave of absence from the fighting, a night in a feather bed. Would that he could sleep again in his old New Orleans bed, sleep in that bed king-sized and crisp and awaken in the morning to the smell of coffee brought to him by a servant; but with nothing like that available here, he made do with this cave, this temporary calm, these wonderfully hot mineral waters that soothed his aching body. Their restorative powers were undeniable, but that did not diminish in the least the admiration he felt for Amoros. The man with the face rounded and soft, strikingly feminine, who had long black hair untouched by any gray — he had been living this life for two decades!

Still, none of that counted now. A critical point had been reached for Amoros, and Waters saw a side of the rebel leader he had never seen before. This was Amoros the irresolute, an Amoros who felt torn between the options he now faced with the Fifty. He felt as if he could harass the army for years if he continued to organize raids and live his life in the highlands, but he also felt that to keep doing that would be to condemn himself to the paltry status of a bandit. Through all the years of struggle, he said, his objective had been for improved social justice on the island, for land reform and an end to the rule by the oligarchy, and it rankled him when his enemies said he was a common outlaw. He could laugh at them, knowing they spoke slander, but the lie irked him nonetheless. In power, he said, with the island's working people behind him, he could institute a spate of reforms. He could decisively alter the conditions on the island. But he would never alter anything here if the US sent in troops.

"They've been the problem since I can remember. Yankee bastards."

The words "Yankee bastards" struck a chord in Jack Waters, but he understood that his definition of the term Yankee and Amoros' allusion to Yankees did not correspond. By Yankee, as an American southerner, he meant someone from up north, someone whose father or uncle or cousin had worn blue in the Civil War, while Amoros meant all Americans, those from the South included. What difference would it make to the rebel leader if American soldiers invading his island hailed from Georgia or Vermont? They were the enemy, to be combatted. But how to preclude that combat was the question, how to seize power and keep them away. The American companies, owning productive island land, in possession of the southern fruit plantations, zealous to maintain the island's staus quo, would object to his plans for reform. So would the foreign businessmen with their money in the casinos. It seemed like he would need a divine intercession to take and hold onto power, unless in power he upheld the status quo and compromised what he hoped to attain. He could perhaps last as president, but he would have to betray the people for whom he'd been fighting.

The rain stopped. Waters and Amoros prepared to leave the cave, loading their horses. Despite their talking and contemplation, they had decided on nothing definite in regard to what the rebels should do next, but Waters marveled at how he of all people had been engulfed by this conflict. He shook his head in disbelief. He was now the main advisor to the leader of the resistance? What of the 34,600 pesos? He couldn't forget that. The General owed him that money. If he never got it from the General but the rebels did take power, he would ask Amoros to give it to him from the island's treasury. This would not be as satisfying as getting the money from Garcia himself, but the payment would be a fair reimbursement in light of the fighting he'd done for the rebels.

They moved out. They spurred their rested horses through the ravine, over the mud and slick rocks, through the white haze of sulfur blowing up from the pools. When they got higher, onto the ridge, the haze cleared, and Waters could see nothing but the forest below them, green as emerald after the rain. Not a tuft of cloud remained in the sky, the sun was strong but not unbearable, and in every direction up above there was the purest, deepest blue. Sometimes, in all this fighting, with his mind fixed on survival, he would forget or go numb to the island's enchantments. He would stop seeing the brilliance of the colors and cease to smell the perfumed flora. But today, riding without pressure, awake to the world after his time holed up in the cave, it stung his eyes to be in the forest, to see the fire of the red flame trees and the orange jacarandas. The soil and trees smelled washed and fresh and the heady rush of aromatic scents — clove trees, soursop, grass, dung, flowers — made him feel giddy. Without question, he said to himself, he was a tropical man. Be he here, or in Louisiana, or somewhere else, he did belong in a tropical place.

Amoros had directed his men where to reconvene when the storm ended. Through the morning and afternoon, he told Waters, the men would come galloping back. Together as a group they could discuss the judiciousness of a full-scale rebel thrust, an all-out attempt to bring down the government, and after that, whatever was decided, they would go ahead and do it. He would lead the fight against the Americans if that was what they wanted.

"You have to be ready to die," he said. "I've been ready these seventeen years."

Up in the hills, at their camp, they found that the men had arrived. But they also found that on their faces the men had expressions like mourners at a funeral. Amoros, swinging down from his horse, asked them what the dejection was about, and Commander Iturbide stepped to the forefront, swishing a sheet of white paper.

"This," he said, tapping the paper, staring at Waters with murder in his eyes. "I guess you haven't seen this."

Somebody else whispered traitor and Iturbide spat through his teeth. He said he had warned everybody, told them not to trust the gringo, and he smiled at the men with the mordancy of one proven right when things are too late.

Waters dismounted and asked to see the note. He put out his hand for the paper, but Iturbide pulled it away. From under a hat of frayed straw he looked at Waters with abhorrence, as if Waters might be a leper, and then he turned his back on him. Others in the group had the note, though — Waters saw it everywhere — and somebody dropped the note to the ground so he could stoop and pick it up.

In astonishment, Waters read the ostensible offer put to him by Hernandez Garcia. He saw the words "payment" and "leave the rebels" and something from the American ambassador about a "guarantee of safety," and he crumpled the note in his fist. He let it slip to the ground. "Screw you," he said, with a derisive smile, but Amoros, standing beside him, had read a copy of the note too, and Waters knew straightaway that it would not be smart for him to deny the implication of the message. He had come and joined the rebels not for a political reason, not to redress social wrongs, but because of a poker debt.

"Yes," he said, addressing the circle, feeling like a man talking in a court. "My initial reason for coming was the debt. The General welshed."

"But you swore you believed in what we're doing."

This from a man in wire glasses, who was eyeing Waters with evident chagrin, and Iturbide answered before Waters could.

"Don't be a fool," Iturbide said. "I told you Dixie here's their pawn."

"I'm nobody's pawn," Waters said. "I never have been. And if I joined you because of the debt, to get my revenge on Garcia, I think my actions since I came have proved my loyalty. I've put my life in danger as much as anybody else here."

"Stand him up against a tree and shoot him," Iturbide said. "Let's get this over with."

Silent through all this, though he looked troubled, was Raoul Cardenes Amoros, and Waters was thinking he was the man that he had to convince. He had to convince the rebel leader that indeed he had changed, that poker and the debt and his old aristocratic comforts were no longer that important to him. Destiny had brought him here to the rebels, had brought him into their battle, and under its guidance he'd changed his life. To kill him now, when inside himself he'd renounced his past, would be too cruel a twist, a way of dying that would be absurd.

"Look at what they're doing," he said. "Can't you see what they're doing? They're trying to raise dissension here by this blatant provocation."

Everybody was yelling, gesticulating, arguing, and Waters could tell the men were hesitant. In his time here with the Fifty, he had become well-liked. He was popular and he had, as he said, put his life in jeopardy as often as anybody else. But Iturbide, his face distended, stuttering in his apoplectic rancor, kept on spouting that he had to be killed. Even if he'd never worked for the enemy, he had lied and abused the group's trust. Iturbide said, as he had before, that gringos, and especially white gringos, and even more especially white gringos from the American South, had no business being on this island.

"I'm not white," Waters said. "You don't know anything about me."

"We know what you are," Iturbide answered.

"No, you don't," Waters said. "My father was white but my mother was a free Creole of color."

"You'll say anything. Like most Americans."

"It happens to be true."

"You never told us before."

171

"How I look should tell you."

"It doesn't."

"It should. If I had my birth documents, I'd show you."

"You're American. Go fight a war in your own damn country. Go start another Civil War. Here with us, what are you but a straggler?"

To Waters this was irrational hatred, unblinking blind hatred, and it did not seem that Iturbide's outlook would ever soften.

"I'm hardly American now," Waters said. "And like I said, I'm not white. I've never owned slaves."

"You would have if you could. If it was allowed."

"But I didn't. The Civil War ended when I was four."

"You still can't be forgiven," Iturbide said.

His eyes were alight and his chubby arms were flexing. Then his right arm tensed and he reached for the gun in his holster. But before he had it out a shot went off, frightfully loud, and Waters watched as Iturbide fell. He drooped to his knees and keeled onto his side, and there he lay without moving, eyes open and looking at him, mouth contorted with lingering hate. In his forehead, there was a hole.

Amoros, holding his own revolver, had shot him.

No one said anything. But every eye in the circle was staring at Iturbide, the dead Iturbide, shot and killed by their leader no less, and Waters sensed that at any second others there might explode. Others there might go for their guns. But would they shoot him or Amoros?

"You. Jack? You'd better get out of here."

Waters heard the words, but they did not register.

"I told you to leave."

It was Amoros telling him this, speaking in a voice weak and quavering, and Waters felt he could not protest without sealing his own death sentence.

Like one impaired, whose limbs were resisting the orders from his brain, he dragged himself over to his horse and lifted himself up into the saddle. He snapped the reins and kicked the piebald's flanks. Then he felt himself riding away, speeding along a forest path, but he had no idea where he would go.

That night, Waters slept in the cave with the sulfur pools. He had ridden here on the minute chance that Amoros would later come, expecting him to seek refuge in this spot. But the next morning, when he awoke, he upbraided himself for his foolishness (Why would Amoros think he'd come here?) and grasped that he was alone. As in the past, when he fled New Orleans, something had happened forcing him to run. He had been cast adrift again. And the image of himself here in this cave, isolated, belonging nowhere, set him thinking about the events of the previous day. What should he make of them? Amoros had shot his own man, a close lieutenant, and all because *he* had been threatened by that man. Amoros hadn't wanted him to die — no question of that — but had the rebel leader reacted out of reflex? Everything had occurred so fast that Amoros might have shot Iturbide without thinking through what he was doing. He had seen Iturbide's gun and fired, that was all. But was it? And now that he had done the unthinkable, shot a longstanding member of the rebels, a loyal member, would his men rebel against him? Waters dearly hoped not, shuddering. He might have caused the downfall of Amoros. Seventeen years the man had been fighting his battles and eluding his enemies, and now, because of him, or because of Amoros' liking for him, the legendary man might have been killed and by none but the resolute men he was leading.

Through the morning and afternoon, Waters brooded in the cave. He had dried pork in his saddle bag and a clump of bananas left in there, and for water he had the limpid streams cascading over stones nearby. As to what he should do or where he should go, he knew he was caught in an awful predicament; if the rebels had rejected him, he was a man as good as dead here. In every town and village he would be spurned, if not knifed or shot by someone, and back in the capital, among his old wealthy acquaintances, he was a wanted man. The wisest thing for him would be to leave, hop a ship out, but to do that here, in so small a place, would be a lot more perilous than it had been in Louisiana. His face here was well-known, he had no means to disguise himself, and if he did find someone to take him, a foreign captain for example, someone in charge of a cargo ship docked at the capital, he would have to pay that man, and as of now he had no money.

Waters sat and continued to brood. He could not believe that fortune had turned against him so abruptly. One day he had been at the center of the cyclone, about to attempt to overthrow the government; the next he was an outcast from everyone. But as a gambler, or a man who had made his living once as a professional gambler, he knew he had to curb his emotions and respond with logic to his difficulties. Between his choices he had to determine which was better, whether to return to the rebels' camp and see if they would take him back or try, somehow, to get off the island. The offer from the General and the invitation from Ambassador Paulsen he didn't consider much, figuring them to be a trap. He would appear at the embassy, asking for the money from the debt, citing their promise of an amnesty, and they would have him arrested and jailed, maybe executed in jail. Of this he had not a shred of doubt.

Even so, come twilight, there he was sitting on his horse and riding through the bush toward the capital. He had resolved, after cogitation, to pay a visit to the US Embassy. But the intent of his visit had nothing to do with accepting the offer crafted to lure him; he was going for a different reason. Waters intended to kill Ambassador Paulsen, kill him and take his head, and afterwards he would ride back to the rebels' camp and gain re-entry into their ranks. How could they turn him away, or deny his commitment to their fight, if he came back with such a prize? Would a double-dealer, an opportunist, shoot the American Ambassador and then bring back his head? No, if he went that far, to such extreme lengths, they would have to let him rejoin them, and he could put to rest once and forever their uncertainty about his motivations.

Not that Waters felt no uneasiness about his plan. The man he'd killed in the French Quarter and the man he'd stabbed at his house — these had been people responsible for the punishments he meted out to them. And here, during raids with the rebels, he had killed and wounded soldiers, but he had done that in battle, in bonafide military situations. Tonight, if he could do it, if he could get to Ambassador Paulsen, he would be killing a man in cold blood, so to speak, committing a premeditated murder, and this was something he himself saw as morally indefensible. However, viewed in the context of the island's fighting, one could say that taking the life of the US Ambassador was also a political move. It would be a blow against the representative of the country supporting the island's government. Ambassador Paulsen, on this island, was a symbol of importance, and so Waters did not feel unjustified plotting the man's assassination.

His ride through the bush went without incident. He'd set out from the cave at dusk, keeping to the lesser-used trails, skirting the villages. And though it was a cloudy night, a night with no moon and dimly shining stars, he never got lost or confused on his trip, secure in his knowledge of the forest, as comfortable in it as a seasoned rebel. He rode in the hope that he would make it back to the men, that Amoros was still alive with them, and before he knew it, he was at the capital. He could see the houses through the trees.

Waters told his horse to stop. He yanked on the reins. He stroked the horse's neck with one hand and let the animal catch its breath. This was the time for him to act, to ride out into the open, but he found himself wavering. It had been weeks — no, months — since he had last been in the capital, and Waters felt strange returning to it. He would have no camouflage here, nothing to use for shelter.

"Hell…Giddy up!"

He took his horse out from the bush and let it trot down the street. The piebald's hooves made no sound in the dirt still moist from the rain. Waters saw no lights and heard no voices coming from the houses he passed; the ornate ones constructed of stone and the flimsy shacks balanced on stilts all looked vacant and ghostly. The only things stirring as he rode through the town were the clothes and sheets hanging from clotheslines, undulating in the night's soft wind, and the occasional dog or rooster foraging through the garbage piles. Yet he did hear noises in the distance, something staccato like the sound of gunfire, and he asked himself whether the rebels might be launching an attack on the capital. Had they agreed on a plan of action since yesterday morning? From his position here in the town, he could not tell where the shooting was coming from, if indeed the noises were shooting, and he made the decision to carry on and try to storm the US embassy.

Outside the mansion, sitting on his horse in the sloping street, he found nothing to impede his access. The elegant white building had no fence or guards, just a flagstone path to the door with a knocker. And when he put his shoulder to the door, having tied his horse to a tree in the yard, he had to hold back a laugh: the knob turned and the door opened. He stepped inside, then stopped in the darkness, adjusting his grip on his Winchester rifle, feeling for the dagger under his shirt. Then he was pushing off again, crossing what appeared to be a foyer, when he had a terrible thought. He smacked his leg. At a set of double doors, he came to a halt. He had the startling realization that he could not do anything worse than kill the United States Ambassador. How could he not have seen this before? If he were to kill Sanford Paulsen, the American government would be furious. It would vow revenge on those responsible. The rebels, who he was doing this for, would be blamed for the assassination, and the full weight of Yankee military might would be brought into play against them. In other words, while Amoros was wracking his brains over how to prevent a US intervention, he would be doing the one thing sure to provoke an intervention. He would deserve to be shot for that.

Deflated, Waters considered retreating, mounting his horse, and riding away. But where? Where could he go? Whether or not the rebels were attacking, he could not risk returning to them, and everybody else on this island was his unqualified enemy.

Beneath the double doors, he could see a flickering light. He could hear no sounds from behind the doors, though, and felt a capricious urge to look in. It was either that or leave the house, go somewhere, and since he could think of nowhere to go, he followed his impulse and moved ahead, flinging back the double doors. He raised his rifle, not knowing what to expect, and saw he was in a wide room staring at a seated woman in black. She had a black shawl over her head and an attractive, sun-bronzed face ribbed by lines of sadness. With her hands bunched under her chin, she was gazing at a young girl laid out in a gown on a long wooden table. There were candles at each end of the table, providing the room's light, and behind the seated woman was somebody else, standing up, an older woman with black skin who was also wearing black.

The woman in the chair looked up and gasped. Her eyes indicated that she recognized him. He had never met the woman before, but he had an idea who she might be.

"Are you Jack Waters?"

"Are you Sanford Paulsen's wife?"

"I am. Isobel Paulsen."

"Well, I'm Jack Waters. But how did you know?"

"You've been, shall we say, described to me."

She was subdued but welcoming in her demeanor, and Waters lowered his rifle. He felt perplexed. He could detect no whiff of menace here, yet the tableau before him, with the girl, dead or sick, lying on the table, was profoundly off-putting. Had he walked in on a funeral service?

Isobel Paulsen said that he had. The girl had been the victim of a violation perpetrated by the President, the corrupt and depraved General Garcia, and rather than see her parents again, rather than go back to them, the girl had hung herself. Mrs. Paulsen said, with grief in her voice, that she had nursed the girl back to health after finding her bleeding in the street, but the shame for the girl had been so terrible that she had ultimately opted for death. Suicide over life for a young girl — horrific — and she wasn't the first Garcia Napoles had molested. Deflowering girls was a ritual for him.

"I've heard about that," Waters said.

He noticed how besides the simple white gown there was a black choker on the girl. He saw with what care she'd been laid out, her black hair combed to cover her shoulders, her arms crossed on her chest. Mrs. Paulsen said that the girl had done something to displease the General while she was in his bed (what that something was she never learned), and instead of getting money to bring home to her parents, as the girls who pleased the General did, she had been expelled from the palace with nothing. And it had been this, the expulsion, the having to go home empty-handed, that had been at the root of her shame. It hadn't been the actual violation, grotesque as that was.

"A ghoul," Mrs. Paulsen said. "The General's a ghoul."

Until this meeting, Waters had known the Ambassador's wife as a name. He knew of her as a cultured woman who moved in the island's upper social brackets, giving and attending parties and banquets. People had told him that her husband was a drunk and she a woman who took lovers. If Waters had ever devoted any thought to Mrs. Sanford Paulsen, it had been with the assumption that she was a wealthy libertine, a woman without much substance to her. He had taken it for granted that her loyalties in this island country must lie with the ruling forces, and the last thing he might have expected was to hear her profess repugnance for the President. But she had, with total conviction, and Waters didn't know what to make of it.

He ventured the statement that he held no love in his heart for the General. In all candor, though, he had never lost sleep over what the man did to young girls; his dislike stemmed from something else.

"*Claro*," Mrs. Paulsen said. "But is that why you came here? To accept the offer in the note?"

"Is that thing genuine?"

"The offer?"

"Yes."

"What's your mind telling you?"

"I'd be an oaf to think it was."

"Then why'd you come here?" Mrs. Paulsen said. "You're taking your life into your hands."

Waters did not answer this, but Mrs. Paulsen was able to interpret his silence. She asked him whether the message in the note had gotten him ostracized from the rebels, and Waters, seeing nothing to lose by acknowledging the truth, said that it had.

"So why'd you come here?" Mrs. Paulsen asked again.

"To be honest…I wanted to kill your husband."

The woman behind Mrs. Paulsen let loose with a laugh, throaty and rich and malevolent, and Waters heard her whisper something in a language that sounded like French.

"Francine says she doesn't blame you one bit," Mrs. Paulsen said. "But my husband's not here now."

The shooting sounds came from the distance, and Mrs. Paulsen said that her husband was over at the palace, trying to defuse the crisis there.

"What crisis?" Waters asked.

"That. The fighting."

The tensions inside the military had come to a head and boiled over. As a result, a coup attempt was in progress. The troops loyal to the General were battling troops organized under the General's principle rival, Colonel Bosch.

"I couldn't care less myself," Mrs. Paulsen said. "We're leaving, Francine and I, after we finish this service. I've had a coffin made and I'll have the girl buried right here on the embassy grounds."

"What about her family?"

"I don't know where they live."

Waters' mind was spinning, toying with a hazy idea, but he needed time to sit down and think. He needed to work his idea out. Mrs. Paulsen, meanwhile, was talking to him again, telling him that in the morning she and Francine would be departing. She had arranged for a ship to take them away, and the ship, packed with their belongings, was waiting for them in the harbor below. At sunrise, they would sail.

"If you want to go with us, you're welcome to," Mrs. Paulsen said. "I don't see why you shouldn't."

Nor could he, since he had no place with the rebels anymore and would likely never collect on his debt. He was fortunate that Mrs. Paulsen, a woman sympathetic toward him, could offer him an escape route.

"Where are you going?" he asked.

"Martinique. It's where we were before we came here, and Francine's home."

Given a stake, money to get started, he could return to gambling there and forget about his ill luck here, how everything had gone wrong for him. And yet, in the darkness of the immense room, as Mrs. Paulsen and the Martinican woman went back to staring at the dead girl, Waters got depressed at the notion of leaving. Much as the rebels might despise him now, he felt he could not run away from them.

He heard the gunshots again and knew in an instant what he had to do. His unformed idea had crystallized.

"Excuse me," he said. "I have to go."

"Go where? Let me tell you where the ship is and you can wait there."

"I'm going back to the bush. To the rebels."

"The rebels!"

"I think I have to try."

Mrs. Paulsen stared at him over the girl's body, her face dark bronze in the candlelight, and he watched her press her fingers together under the point of her chin.

"You want to help them," she said. "I'll be...it's not the debt anymore."

"It was nice meeting you," Waters said.

He turned on his heel but she asked him to wait. She got up and came around the table in her black mourning dress.

"What will they do if you go back?"

"I don't know," Waters said. "Maybe shoot me."

"This is a time when the rebels could defeat the army."

It was something he couldn't believe she'd said, implying that she knew his aims and shared them, and Waters asked for elucidation. Could she state more clearly what she meant?

"If the rebels were to strike tonight," she went on, "with the army split and disorganized…Is that what you were thinking?"

"I wasn't thinking anything," Waters said. "But I do have to go."

"Then I'm coming with you."

"You what?"

"I'm changing my clothes, saddling up, and coming with you. I can ride a horse."

"That's madness."

"Why? From you, with your status, the rebels won't believe a word you say when you say now's the time to attack. But from me, the Ambassador's wife… Would they believe it's a trap? I don't think so."

Waters did not know what they would think, or do, but if she was so insistent on coming, he would lead her into the bush. From the Ambassador's wife herself the rebels would hear they had a chance to snatch power now, when their enemies were fighting internecine skirmishes. But would her appearance in the forest be too shocking for them? How could they trust her, the American Ambassador's wife, on anything? They couldn't, but she would be putting herself at their mercy by coming out to their camp. Amoros and the others would have to take that into account. This could be the occasion for Amoros to make the decisive move to grab power, and to hell with worrying about what might happen with the US. He himself could say to Amoros that this was the chance to avoid the fate of being seen as a bandit forever.

An hour later, he was back on his horse, pounding through the night and the forest again. He had Mrs. Paulsen behind him, wearing boots, white breeches, and a black jersey, her hair held under an equestrian cap, and as she had said to him in the mansion, she could ride as well as anyone.

"All these years living in the tropics, you think I can't ride a horse?"

They had gotten one, a chestnut colt, from out of the embassy's stables, and the man who took care of the horses there had put on the saddle and bridle. Then Mrs. Paulsen had run back into the house, into the room with the girl on the table, and she asked her servant Francine to leave as planned by the ship in the harbor.

"Madame...Don't."

"I have to," Mrs. Paulsen said. "I must. But if I'm not back by noon tomorrow — give me till noon — go to Martinique without me."

"*C'est fou*, madame!"

"And you'll have to oversee the girl's burial. I don't want to lose another second."

She told the stable manager, who had dug the grave on the embassy lawn, to lower the girl into the ground, and then she and Waters had ridden off.

The night was clearer than before, less cloudy, with the moon throwing shafts of light in the bush. And even though they were riding fast, Mrs. Paulsen had a great deal to say. It seemed that she had a remorseful conscience. For all these years, she said, she had been living hedonistically, ignoring crimes going on around her, and what the General had done to that girl had driven home these facts. She could never bring the girl back to life but if she could do something, anything, to make up for her years of blindness...

"And your husband?" Waters asked. "How would he feel about what you're doing?"

The laughing snort she gave as an answer told of her disdain for him, and she characterized the man as useless. He was an alcoholic most himself when he was lying drunk in his hammock.

"He kept on carping about my taking in the girl. How it would not sit well with the General, the dear, dear General…"

Waters didn't want to remind her that what she was doing might be judged a treasonous act by the American government. Yet he did feel duty bound to tell her that she was putting her life at risk by going out to the rebels. They might choose to kill her or take her as a hostage for ransom, but he heard her say she knew all that and was not about to be frightened off.

"They might kill you, too," she said.

"They might."

"So. We'll have to see what happens."

Waters grunted out a "Yeah, we will," and after that they spoke little while riding hard, while pushing their horses, while traveling up toward the rebels' territory.

THE GLORY OF HISTORY

Weeks after the fighting ended, when the rebels had taken power and Raoul Cardenes Amoros had declared himself president, moving into the palace, the United States military forces still had not invaded the island. Amoros himself could scarcely believe this, though on his first day in power he'd dispatched a telegram to the American president, Theodore Roosevelt. In it he stated his desire to have good relations with Washington, and he asserted that there was no reason for the "big stick" to come down on the island since he had his nation under control. The whole purpose of his takeover, he said, had been to force out a corrupt dictator who was running the country for his own profit and leaving most of the people in squalor. And he insisted that though he intended to enact reforms, he did not have any plans or wishes to interfere with American businesses operating on the island.

Help in the wording of this message had come from none other than Isobel Paulsen. She emphasized the need for him to sound conciliatory toward Washington. At the same time, using stealth and cunning, he could bring about his reforms. It would be no easy job ruling under the eye of the Yankees, but he would have to find a balance between keeping them off his back and not seeming to betray his followers, the ordinary peasants and rebel combatants who had routed the disorganized army in the last days of the recent fighting.

Soldiers for the army were dead, in jail, or had fled the island. General Garcia had sailed away, too (either to Spain or Venezuela, nobody knew for sure), and with him had gone chests full of money kept inside the palace. As for Colonel Bosch, whose men had been battling the General's men when the rebels attacked the palace, he had been killed during the fighting, and his body was buried in an unmarked grave with the bodies of other military personnel.

There was rejoicing in the highlands and among the workers on the haciendas. Those not rich and living in the capital applauded the change of regimes also. But nearly all the landowners staunchly opposed Raoul Amoros, the man who had been their worst enemy for the last seventeen years, and without the army to enforce their dictates, they had to seek support from the Yankees. In their view, the Marines were needed. If the American soldiers were to come, normalcy could be re-established and a government of their choosing installed.

This is where Isobel came in again, with her diplomatic experience. At Amoros' behest, esteemed by him and the rebels after her role in the overthrow, she was the one who met with the managers of the American fruit plantations. Her husband Sanford had given up, calling her turn to the rebels imprudent, swearing that he was through with the island and his position in the foreign service. He was sullen and bleary-eyed and never left the embassy residence except to go to bars and drink. Soon, in a week or so, the new ambassador would arrive, but in the interim she was acting as such, meeting with American nationals at the embassy or traveling to American-owned areas by horseback. When she left the capital, Amoros' men would escort her. The Americans saw this retinue as significant, and she told her fellow citizens nothing would change for them. She informed them that the US military had its eye on everything; the USS Gold Mine, a protected cruiser, had sailed over from Dominican waters and anchored in the harbor. You could see the ship from the embassy balcony and the capital's shoreline. Charles Grant, a bald-scalped military attache, had come aground, and over a lunch at the residence, he'd let her know that Marines were on the ship, ready for action if needed. But Grant stressed that the troops were there to safeguard American interests, not to sweep across the island. They wouldn't come ashore unless forced to. The truth was that the Administration had grown tired of Garcia, and it thought that stability might come to the island if Amoros could be held on a leash. He was someone with broad popular backing, and that could mean a calmer island. Under Garcia, who was corrupt and incompetent, the island had been sliding toward anarchy, and so the US government was prepared to give Amoros a chance despite his years as an insurgent.

"What you did that night," the attache said. "On your own? Could have been a disaster."

"But it wasn't."

"No."

"Tell my husband that."

"He needs a rest."

"He'll get one when he leaves."

"Next week?"

"That's right," Isobel said.

"And you?"

"I'll relay what you said to Amoros."

"I've spoken with him," the attache said. "He knows we're watching him close, but if he doesn't rock the boat, we won't toss him."

The rebels had not damaged any Yankee plantations in years, and Amoros promised that his men wouldn't go near them now. So the troops on the Gold Mine kept to the ship, which stayed in the harbor, and the island's moneyed complained of betrayal. The Americans, they said, were nothing if not two-faced. Of the outcomes that might have resulted from Garcia's fall, the landowners could not cotton to this — the gringos letting Amoros rule.

For Jack Waters, these developments were of scant interest. Though gratified the rebels had won, he was happy to be done with the fighting and done with the day-to-day world of the rebels. He felt he'd reconciled with them the night he'd ridden back to them and passed along the information that different factions of the island's army were absorbed in fighting each other. Yet that had been Isobel's night, and she had done the better part of the talking. She'd amazed him with her persuasiveness. He had stood by and held his tongue as she told Amoros and the rebels that her visit alone was proof that she meant no deception; they need only kill her if what she was saying was untrue.

"You can kill both Waters and me. But if you strike fast, the army can be beaten."

They'd sent men to reconnoiter, keeping Isobel with them at their camp, and when those scouts backed up what she said, the fateful assault had been made. By its end, everybody knew what they were doing and not just the men in The Fifty were fighting. People from all over the island had joined them. And Waters was there in the thick of it, running through f and using his rifle, smelling the blood and dead bodies.

The mishap with Commander Iturbide, regrettable as it had been, was not held against him by anyone. His rebel cohorts forgot that event for the sake of unity, and even to those once skeptical about him, he'd proven himself. Waters moved into the hotel he had stayed at earlier, before his days living in the bush. Despite the stories connected to his name, what had become his fearsome reputation, the hotel manager let him come back. In that man's memory,

Waters was a well-mannered boarder who had never lagged in paying his bill. He gave Waters the airy room he had resided in the last time, and Waters paid him for the upcoming month. Waters had the money he'd received after the occupation of the palace; he'd asked Amoros to take from the treasury the 34,600 pesos that the departed General owed him. And though Amoros said that the treasury had been looted by the General, he agreed to give Waters the money. Out in the palace courtyard, he handed him a roll of cash. But he hoped Waters was appreciative; none of The Fifty's other men would be getting money from the treasury. Their sole reward for the long struggle would have to be the victory itself.

"I can't build roads or get anything done if I don't have the money."

"I understand that," Waters said. "But I was owed this money."

"By Garcia. Not by me."

"It's a fair settlement."

"For who? My government? But I know you didn't start fighting with us because you believed in our cause."

"I just wish we'd got Garcia."

"Me, too. But are you satisfied?"

"Yes."

"You should be."

So Waters had come full circle. He found himself back where he'd been before joining the rebels. But when he was honest with himself, he could admit to disgruntlement. More than he'd let on to Amoros, he simmered over Garcia's escape. He'd wanted that man to pay him, no one else. He'd envisaged Garcia groveling before him, begging for his life while holding out the money, and he'd reckoned on being on the firing squad that would execute Garcia after the revolution. None of that had occurred, and to top it off, Waters had less money now than in his pre-rebel days. The savings he'd relinquished when he came to the rebels exceeded the debt itself. But he'd lived up to his paramount principle — intolerance for welshers — and he could not deny that the rebels triumph meant something to him. Never before in his solitary life had he been immersed in something larger than himself. Never before had he fought for something beyond his own concerns. He felt he'd done what his father had when serving the Confederates in the Civil War. But unlike his father he'd survived, lived through the battles, and he intended to resume his life where he'd left off months ago — playing poker for high stakes.

Waters discerned an impediment, though. The people he'd formerly gambled with had become his enemies. They were the islanders who owned haciendas, the people whose estates he'd raided with The Fifty. Nobody would ever again invite him to their mansions to play poker. And then there were the island's casinos, owned by foreigners, but these had all shut down temporarily due to the political turmoil. None of the casino owners knew where they stood with Raoul Amoros. Did he want to close the casinos? Would they have to pay him off? Garcia had let them run their places while taking a quarter of their daily profits. They were waiting to meet with Amoros to talk everything over. But even if he did let them keep operating, Waters knew it might not matter. The casinos were private enterprises and the casino owners, friends of the island's aristocrats, might ban him from their premises. At bottom, he had cut himself off from the class of people he needed to know to make money, and he could not see them extending an olive branch.

On his next visit to the presidential palace, Waters brought this up. He met with Raoul Amoros in the office where Garcia had held court, and he did find it disconcerting to be looking at the rebel leader seated behind a massive desk. In his physical appearance, Amoros was unchanged — thin, wearing black clothes, his hair neck-length and combed behind his ears — but something inside him seemed altered. Despite the arduousness of his life, Amoros had been at home in the bush. Intimacy with its paths and nooks had bred self-possession in him. Here however, in an office, enclosed by walls and furniture, Amoros looked edgy. Ramrod stiff in the chair behind his desk, he kept fiddling with a nail clipper. His eyes would stray to the window, and the sun beyond it, and Waters imagined he might do better to run his government from somewhere else. Outside the capital, if he set up an office in a village, he might feel less out of place.

"I'll get used to it," Amoros said. "And you, without your poker?"

"Without that, I have no income."

Amoros asked whether that would be a bother to him.

"Not having an income?"

"Not playing cards."

"Cards are my love and profession. I have to get back to it."

Waters recalled his game with the General and the mistreatment he'd received. He remembered the times after that game when he'd tried to re-enter the palace to ask Garcia for money. The General's minions had shunted him away, and Waters had to say to himself that it felt pleasing to return to the palace. Ensconced in a chair facing the desk, he arched his back and stretched his legs. He felt unabashedly proud of himself for having helped oust Garcia. But the country's new leader, behind his desk, seemed to be sharing none of his joy, and Waters began to feel nervous. He pulled in his legs. Amoros was looking at him as if he'd disclosed he'd robbed a bank.

"Have I said something wrong?" Waters asked.

Amoros said that he had. He said that the fighting might be over but now the real work would begin. Keeping and consolidating power while trying to achieve reforms on the island would be a monumental task, and for Waters to come to him complaining about a dearth of card games was a supreme waste of his time.

"I haven't decided about the casinos," Amoros said. "I'm not sure what I'll do with them. But if you can't find poker here, you can go somewhere else. Cuba or Martinique."

Waters shot back that he liked the island and did not want to move again.

"Then work with us in what we're doing. I have any number of jobs you could do. But don't expect me to pass a law ordering people to play cards with you."

Waters was beginning to feel that something between him and Amoros had soured. And Amoros asked him whether he retained his commitment to The Fifty. He'd been thinking Waters had changed, but the Jack Waters talking today sounded like the old Jack Waters, a Yankee who had come to this island because it had everything he wanted. It had cheap living, hot weather, casinos, rum, and hunting, and he could use it as his personal paradise.

"I'm not a Yankee, dammit."

"You are an American, and you've started to act like one again."

"Is it a sin to do what I love? To want to do it?"

"It's not a sin, no."

"And poker's what I'm good at."

"You helped a revolution and our country. We can make things better for people."

"Yes…"

"You've done something for history," Amoros said.

"History? Big word."

"It's true."

"I never said I'm noble."

"You don't have to be," Amoros said.

"What would you have me do then?"

"I told you. Help us with the work we have."

Amoros suggested he leave his hotel and move into a room in the palace. Other ex-rebels were in the palace and soon he'd be assigning them government posts. To Waters he could offer something he'd like, something outdoors and not at a desk (a farm and plantation inspector once he introduced his land reform plan on non-American property), and he could promise decent pay. Waters would not get rich at this job, but he would be helping the revolution.

In reply, Waters balked. He balked at the notion of regular labor just as he had in New Orleans. There, rather than tend his fertile estate or lease it out to sharecroppers, he had let the land grow wild. And he still saw himself as a man of leisure, somebody from the aristocratic class, and did not think he should have to work if he could live well by gambling. He apprehended that on this island he had been fighting *against* the aristocrats, but something inside him clung to the belief that he was an independent entity, beholden to no one. He'd given himself to the rebels' cause, true enough, but that was because it had dovetailed with his own. Proud as he was of his role in the conflict, he had never meant to spend his life entangled in the island's political affairs.

"Thanks for the offer," he told Amoros. "Lemme think on it."

He went back to his hotel room, back to the four heat-smudged walls. From exultant over the rebels win, he had become disheartened, and for what remained of the day he sat in his sweltering room and drank. The rum gave him a headache, though, and made him sweat profusely, and when the evening breeze came on, he requested a bath drawn for himself and asked that the water not be warmed. The hotel servants brought a big metal basin and placed it on the floor in his room, then they filled it up with buckets, running to and from a well in the courtyard. As he lay cooling off, alone again, his arms up on the basin's rim, he listened to the whir of the crickets outside and tried to forget his meeting with Amoros. But he could not. The strain in their relations upset him. He ran a thumb through the bathwater and thought back to the mineral baths he and Amoros had taken together in that highland cave. Their time in the highlands, stinging the army and raiding haciendas, keeping on the move and setting up camps, already seemed long ago, and Jack Waters put it to himself that maybe he should do what Amoros said and pursue his card playing elsewhere.

He rode his piebald, he went bird hunting, he dropped in on village bars where people greeted him with smiles. But there was reserve in these smiles, and nobody would ask him over to their table or strike up a conversation with him. The bartenders served him and moved away, and people he knew, men he'd fought with, turned their backs on him at the counters. What was happening? In spite of the courteousness shown him, the atmosphere of glacial civility reminded him of being back home and walking into certain bars. These were whites-only bars, where he could pass for a white person, but people might suspect, from the tincture of brown in his skin, that his background was mixed. Or they might know, if they knew his family history. People would go cold to him, shun him while he drank, but their coldness seemed daft to Waters. His experience told him neither whites nor blacks were more or less trustworthy than the other. As he'd told somebody once, he would sit at a table and play cards with whites or blacks as long as they had the money for the game and did their gambling without cheating. It was funny, but his ease with blacks had led some back home, who didn't know he was mixed, to call him a nigger lover. Waters would say no to the charge; he'd enlighten them; he'd explain he loved no mass of people, black or white. To his way of thinking, it was every man for himself and God against all, though on this island that motto appeared to have a variation. Here, every person, rich and poor, white and black, had fallen into line against him.

The exception to this was Isobel Paulsen. He'd been on convivial terms with her since the night they met. More and more often in his isolation, Waters would visit her at the embassy, and they would sit out on the veranda with the French windows open behind them. They would sit there in the evenings pouring drinks for themselves, and when they were not saying anything, they'd hear the rollers breaking against the harbor wall.

Aside from the local house girl, Isobel had the mansion to herself. Francine had returned home to Martinique, and her husband, the alcoholic, had done what he'd been threatening to do for months. Not inclined to wait for his replacement, he'd deserted his post as US ambassador and snuck away in the dead of night to board a ship sailing out. Nobody knew which ship he'd taken, but Isobel felt it must have been a ship bound for Europe. Being in France or Italy, going to the opera there, circulating among what he saw as the refined class, was what he wanted for himself, and his failure to live this life had accounted for his incessant railing about being sent to the tropics. The last straw had been the rebellion and how Isobel had worked against him, and these combined with the US government ignoring his dispatches asking for troops had convinced him that he had no future in the American foreign service.

"In Europe," Isobel said, "he can drink all he wants in high style."

"Until when?" Waters said.

"Till his money runs out."

"And then?"

"Then I don't know," Isobel said, and though she smiled, her eyes were sad.

Waters and Isobel talked about their lives before their days on the island. They discussed how their lives had changed here. And sometimes, when they did not talk, Isobel played the piano for Waters. In lightweight slacks and a ruffle-necked blouse she would sit at the keyboard while he reclined on the blue chaise lounge in the room off the veranda. She would perform a Mozart sonata or *The Maple Leaf Rag*. She would sit on the bench with her back straight and her head tilted forward, and to look at this gravely dynamic woman with her reddish-brown hair and dark eyes made Waters reflect on his solitary life. He would ask himself why he'd never wanted to marry, why he'd never found love. The only woman he had ever been close to was his mother, and the bulk of his other time with women had been spent with prostitutes. His mother had been the most dominant person in his life, raising him alone and teaching him how to play poker, and he wondered whether her presence in his mind had checked him from striking any bonds with women. Or had his limited dealings with women, his whorehouse dealings, come about because of his obsession with gambling? Fixated on poker, he had never much missed having a romantic life, but out of the nowhere sitting here with Isobel, he felt himself to be incomplete.

He sought nothing from Isobel herself but did admire her. He saw her as a kindred exile. But she was someone who seemed more content in her state of exile than he did in his, and when he asked her what her plans were, she said she would stay at the embassy residence until the new ambassador arrived. Then she would take a house in town and begin work writing a book Raoul Amoros had commissioned.

"A book?" Waters asked.

"On Amoros' life, the history of The Fifty, and the fall of Hernandez Garcia."

"A book?" He could not give credence to what he was hearing.

"Yes? So?"

"I didn't know you write in Spanish."

"It'll be in English," Isobel said. "It's for publication in the States, to help people know him there. By knowing him, they can understand what he's done and what he's doing."

She would shelve the novel she'd started because this book took precedence. If it could help Amoros in any way, if it could help the revolution, it was worth writing.

"Don't you feel you should help?" she asked.

Waters had to smile. "You've been talking to Amoros," he said.

"I might have."

"What'd he say?"

"That you two have a rift."

"That's his word — 'rift'? Okay. It's a rift."

He defended his right to decline Amoros' job offer, but Isobel said he should follow the President's words. He should leave the island or work on behalf of the government. For him to stay and ramble around, playing cards if and when he had the opportunity, would be a snub to everyone he'd fought with. It came as no surprise that Amoros was angry with him, and she reminded him that in the forest Amoros had saved his life and jeopardized his own life doing it.

"You know about that?" Waters asked.

"Everyone does," Isobel said. "Haven't you learned it's a small island?"

He'd disappointed Amoros, she said. If he had killed his own man to protect him, then there must have been a time when the rebel leader held him in high regard. So how did he expect Amoros to react to his disengagement from the fight? As an outsider herself, she could understand why he was hoping to bow out of the island's politics and slip back into his old lifestyle, but she did think that without a commitment to the revolution, he should go.

"Try Martinique," Isobel said. "I can cable the ambassador."

"You know him?"

"Well. And I'll get you introductions."

"Maybe I will," Waters said. "Maybe I will."

He left indignant. As he walked back to his hotel, dampened by a sea wind, eyes looking down at the night's shadows, he ruminated over the trickiness of fate. Isobel, who had fought with the rebels precisely one night, had been appointed the revolution's English language historian, while he, their cohort for months, had wound up a pariah. Raoul Amoros had mentioned history to him and how by joining the rebels he'd done something for history, but was this how history repaid him? By alienating him, for the second time now, from his comrades in arms? Why should he respect history? In the form of a war it had killed his father when he was an infant, despoiled the land he came from, and left his mother a melancholy widow who exhausted herself bringing him up. It had let General Garcia Napoles escape the agonizing death Waters wanted to give him. History was the word people used when they hoped to lend meaning to the arbitrary workings of chance, and if Isobel's ascension to chronicler of the revolution and his slide back to island outcast didn't support this view, he didn't know what did.

His finances dwindling, Waters knew he had to make a decision. Self-respect and his love of poker said he should leave the island, but sentiment disagreed. He'd given his sweat and blood to this place like he never had anywhere else. At home a rash act had necessitated flight, but now he'd be running because he couldn't bear to accept a job in lieu of playing cards.

It seemed peevish. He'd start a new life again, and for what? He had a friend here, Isobel, and felt that if he took the work Amoros gave him, his one-time compatriots would take him back into their fold. Out of contrariness alone, he should accept Amoros' offer. He should say yes to show his detractors, Amoros among them, that he could submit himself to a cause. He knew what "selfless" meant.

It took him five days to secure a meeting with Amoros. The two times he went to the palace to ask admittance, the guards stationed outside the spike-topped fence said he would have to wait, that he should come back. That they were men he'd fought alongside galled him, and their blockage prompted memories of when he'd attempted to get inside the palace to request his poker winnings from Garcia Napoles. Talk about history! It was repeating itself, though Waters did not see himself going to the extremes he had before. His pursuit of a job would not lead him to take up arms against Amoros.

He sped back to the embassy mansion, and over rum and cane syrup cocktails, he asked Isobel whether she could shed light on Amoros' thinking. He'd given a note to a palace guard stating he'd accept a position and work for the revolution, no strings attached, but

Amoros remained silent and unreachable. Was the President busy, or avoiding him? Had he exasperated Amoros so much in their earlier talk that Amoros had written him off? Neither in the bush while fighting nor since Amoros had become president had he ever had to wait to speak to him.

"I don't get it," Waters said. "If his offer's gone and he wants me to leave, after all we've been through, he should tell me."

"I don't think it's that," Isobel said.

"What then?"

"You'll have to talk to Amoros."

"You must have some idea."

Isobel said she'd heard through the grapevine that the arriving ambassador, a Mr. Edward Sewell, had cabled Amoros about him.

"Edward Sewell? Should I know who he is?"

"He's a career diplomat."

"And?"

"And he may have an interest in you. I'm not privy to what the cable said."

Sewell was the name Waters had on his mind when he returned to his hotel that evening, and after the summons from the palace came, through a note slipped under his door at daybreak, Sewell and his telegraph wire were the first things Waters spoke of when he met Amoros in his office.

"Yes," said Amoros. "He'll be ashore by the end of the week."

"What's the connection to me starting work?"

The contours in Amoros' face had hardened, the hair at his temples was turning white. The presidency was aging him in ways years of warfare had not.

"I have to talk to Sewell about it."

"Why?"

"I have to."

"If you don't want me for the job anymore…"

"I'd take you," Amoros said. "It's Sewell."

"*What's* Sewell?"

"He wants me to put you in prison till he gets here."

"Prison?" Waters said. He felt heat behind his eyes, constriction in his chest. "He doesn't know me."

"He represents your government."

"Of course he does. But if the Americans accept the overthrow…"

"This isn't about your part in the overthrow."

"Then what?"

"The man you killed back home," Amoros said. "The man in Louisiana. They want to take you back for that."

Stupefied, Waters sat down. He felt a tremor in his chest. He put his hands on the chair's hardwood arms, and as he tried to digest what he'd heard, Amoros shut the door to the hall and positioned himself against his desk, stern-looking in his green tunic. Amoros said that he was sorry, but through Ambassador Edward Sewell he'd found out that tales of Waters' exploits on the island had gotten back to New Orleans and the father of the man he'd killed at his house. It was Sanford Paulsen, weeks ago, who had cabled the authorities there asking whether they had information on a person with his name, and from that point on, the die had been cast. A sheriff had told the victim's father of his whereabouts, and this man, wealthy and powerful, a businessman with high connections, had gone then to government officials to see about getting him extradited.

"That scum had a father?" Waters said.

"You didn't know him well?"

"First time we'd played."

"Whatever he was, he came from money."

"The man didn't teach his son very much."

"Unless he's like him."

"And you'd really do it?" Waters asked. "You'd hand me over?"

"I may have to," Amoros said.

"How's that?"

"A sign of good faith with your government."

"Stop saying *my* government."

"You didn't want to help ours."

"I did help. Have you forgotten everything?"

"You helped the revolution," Amoros said. "I'm talking about after that."

"I said yes. I'll accept the post."

"You just said that. If you'd said it earlier, maybe I could tell Mr. Sewell you're an official member of my government. But you're not, and it's too late now."

Waters thought of Isobel's admonition that he go to Martinique and resume his life playing poker there, and he told Amoros he would do as she counselled. With him gone, Amoros could more comfortably face the Americans. The father of the cheater, if he had the will, could pursue him to Fort de France. Waters would be waiting for him. He didn't want to leave after the risks he'd taken during the fighting and the sacrifices he'd made, but if political obligations, abhorrent as they were, left him no choice, he'd say goodbye and board a ship. He'd know he had contributed something to the island.

"Can't do it," Amoros said. "They'd think I let you escape."

"Tell them I sailed before you gave the order to hold me."

"They won't believe that."

Was this the same Raoul Amoros who'd fought so long against an oppressive government? The American backing for that government had let Hernandez Garcia Napoles survive as long as he did, and now Amoros was following in that toady's footsteps.

"You're becoming a pawn," Waters said.

"What did you say?"

"Let's go back to the cave," Waters said. "Talk this over there, away from everything. There has to be a solution."

Amoros raised himself off his desk, his face granite. He croaked something unintelligible, rubbed his throat, and closed his eyes. So far as Waters could tell, he was either enjoying an agreeable memory of the cave, with its mist and sulfur pools, or he was trying to forget the days they had spent there together. Waters didn't want to ask which, however, and he waited for Amoros to open his eyes.

"I have a country to run, Waters. A country! And you want me to go back to the cave with you?"

"To strategize. Like we used to. There has to be a way to handle this."

"Guards!"

The door to Amoros' office opened, and three men with rifles entered. They were men Waters knew, men who'd been rebels. Though scraggly-bearded when in the bush, each had shaved off his whiskers since, and on their blotchy hairless faces there were regretful looks. One held a rope.

"You can't do this," Waters said. "I helped you win your war."

As they walked him through town, Waters kept his chin up and his eyes straight ahead. He had a guard to his left, a guard to his right, and the third behind him. His wrists were bound in front of him, down by his waist. He felt the midday sun on his back, pasting his shirt to his skin, and a brutal thirst. The bones in his feet hurt, as did his wrists, chafed by the ropes. The guards were handling him like a criminal, demeaning him in public, but he disregarded passers-by — the men on horses, half-clad children, a gaping woman with white hair and no teeth. Had these people ever seen a gringo bound and helpless, being led to jail? Didn't they know that if not for him, the fight against Garcia might still be going? Waters felt sure they knew of his feats, his importance to the over-throw, yet nobody said a word to him. Nobody asked the guards why he'd been arrested.

Waters blamed Amoros. It had become clear that one president was as perfidious as another, but though he had avenged himself on General Garcia Napoles, the most he could do in this case was effect a stoical front. He put on his blandest poker countenance. He asked no questions and showed no discomfort and vowed that he'd go to his prison cell in silence. Or if the promise of jail was a lie, made to keep him calm while they led him to his execution, for whatever reason they had devised to kill him, he would, despite that, say nothing. If the guards stood him up against a wall to shoot him, he'd refuse the blindfold and spit at them. He'd cock his head toward the sky while they aimed.

"Viva the Revolution!" he'd shout, and by that he'd mean the real fight, the one against all the world's backstabbers, its cheaters and opportunists, the power-hungry and hypocritical.

His prison cell had one window, with bars but no glass, overlooking the harbor. When his guards had freed him and left him alone, slamming the cell's iron door and turning its lock behind them with a clank, he climbed up on the wooden stool there and wrapped his fingers around the bars. The jail was a converted military fortress the Spaniards had built when they owned the island, so it stood on a hill above the harbor from where it had once loomed as a bulwark against invading fleets, the English and French. Waters could see the funnels and masts of the USS Gold Mine, anchored about half a mile offshore, and beyond that was the open sea, light blue until the horizon. To survey that space, the mirror-flat water below and the cloudless sky above, inflamed him no end, and feeling he would neither be seen nor heard, he cut loose a barrage of imprecations that called for Amoros to die. He had never felt so impotent. People were outside the jail, he thought, out in the city and forest, in the fields and their villages, going about their everyday lives, and he through no fault of his own was trapped in this cell and waiting for...what? The arrival of the US ambassador? He had better come with support, thought Waters, because the son of a bitch wasn't taking him anywhere without him putting up a fight.

Sundown came, then darkness. Waters lit the gas lamp on the cell's bare table. He had a pail to use for a toilet and a rectangle of metal slats for a bed. If he stood at one wall and walked eight paces across the floor, he reached the opposite wall, and to occupy himself he had nothing except the deck of cards a sentry had brought from his hotel room. Amoros, or the warden, had ordered the delivery of his rucksack. He could wear his clothes and he had his possessions around him minus his rifle, knife, and razor. He ate the gruel the jailors gave him for breakfast, the black beans and rice they slid through the door slot for lunch and dinner. A bump on the floor signaled when meal time was over, and he would have to put the bowl, his water cup, and the spoon on the floor by the opening. "Done," he'd say, and two hands would shoot through the slot and take everything.

With the one window, the cell proved unrelentingly hot. Day after day, Waters slept to get through it, lying in his perspiration. He could sleep or play solitaire to pass the time, and he preferred to sleep because he could dream. His mind pulsed with dreams. In most he could remember, he was in the past, back home on his estate, sitting bedside by his mother in her white nightgown, her gray hair covering the bed like the tendrils of a plant, or he was riding his jet-black colt across land green and swampy. Why had he let that land go savage? He could have cultivated it, he'd think. He would ride so fast through the weeds and cypresses he would feel as if he was weightless.

Four days went by. Waters counted them. He worried he'd lose track of time as prisoners in solitary could. The end of the week, when the ambassador was slated to arrive, had to be soon, and one sweltry morning, when he heard keys jangling outside his cell, it seemed that the inevitable had come. He sat up in bed. A key went in the door, a lock gear rasped, and the door swung inward, but he saw not the guards, as he was expecting, or an American diplomat or even Raoul Amoros. His visitor was Isobel Paulsen, and she told the sentry holding the keys he could leave her alone with Waters.

"He won't hurt me."

"How can you know?"

"He won't."

"I have to lock the door behind you."

"I'll be safe," Isobel said.

She had black boots and white riding clothes on, and a black top hat, with a tulle rear veil, covered her hair. Stubbly and unwashed, in soiled clothes, Waters knew he looked and smelled revolting, and nothing could mask the stink from his waste bucket.

"I've had better accommodations," he said.

"I wish this hadn't happened."

"My arrest? It didn't have to."

He stayed on the bed, his feet on the floor, but offered her the stool to sit. She lifted the stool, crossed his cell, and put it under the window. "Can you see the harbor from here?" she said, crooking her leg, getting up onto the stool. "Uh-huh. I thought so." And she stuck her hand, palm up, through the bars.

"What?" Waters asked. "I should have listened to you and left?"

"The USS Gold Mine. The Americans."

"What about them?"

"They're a fact we can't ignore," Isobel said. "If Amoros tries to ignore them..."

"He's knuckling under and it didn't take him long in power to do that."

Isobel stepped down from the stool but did not sit. Her hands on her hips, she angled her head, not meeting his eyes with her own.

"He's being realistic," she said. "If he doesn't deal, give them some things they want, he can't get anything done for everyone else."

"And I'm a thing they want."

"Sanford's the one who cabled New Orleans about you being here. I'm truly sorry for that."

"Sorry, sorry, sorry," Waters said. "Doesn't get me out of here, does it?"

Isobel said they had to go to the palace, where the ambassador and Amoros were waiting for him, but that the prison guards would bring him water so he could clean himself first.

"I'll wait outside."

"You're my escort?"

"You'll have guards. I thought you wouldn't mind if I walk with you, though."

"Always nice to see a dead man, isn't it?"

At the palace, in the president's office, Amoros was sitting at his desk and a man was seated across from him in a black tuxedo. He had a white mustache and a Van Dyke beard, and his long-chinned face was studious. The guards had gone, leaving Waters unshackled, but Isobel came into the room. She introduced Waters to the man — "This is Edward Sewell, the American Ambassador." — and told Waters to take a chair so they could discuss their business. Waters sat, not seeing what else he could do, but behind his docility, he was considering making a run and leaping through the office's window. They *had* freed his hands. But how far would he get if he broke through the glass and ran for it? Where would he go? He'd need to get past the sentries and fence surrounding the palace, and Amoros himself had to have a pistol in his desk drawer. An old fighter like him, even sitting here in civilian clothes, black pants and a guayabera shirt, never let himself be without a gun. If given a reason, would Amoros actually shoot him?

The ambassador was talking:

"Jack Waters, I have the papers for your extradition."

As laid out by Sewell, the transfer plan was uncomplicated; two members of the island's army, men trusted by Amoros, would take Waters to Louisiana on a commercial steamer. The ship had reached port here two days ago and would depart for New Orleans in three. While they waited for it to sail, Waters would remain in prison.

"I don't even merit house arrest?" Waters asked.

"I'd feel safer with you in the prison," Sewell answered.

"President Amoros?" Waters said, trying to keep from sounding sarcastic. "You'd feel safer with me there, too?"

"No..."

As if Waters had slapped him, Amoros blanched, and he stood up from his chair with such violence, the chair fell over backwards. Sewell drew himself up also. He tugged at the hem of his jacket and readjusted his bowtie. His body convulsing, he coughed into his hand. To all indications, the parley was finished, and Ambassador Sewell asked Amoros to ring for the men who'd return Amoros to prison.

"No prison," Amoros said. "House arrest will do."

Sewell coughed again, like one tubercular.

"I don't understand, Mr. President."

"House arrest till the ship is ready to leave."

"That wasn't our agreement."

"I said you'll get him and you will."

"When?" Sewell asked.

"When it's time for the ship to sail."

"The authorities in New Orleans expect him."

'You've told me," Amoros said.

"We don't want to get off on the wrong foot."

"We won't."

"Your government and mine."

"We'll send him back," Amoros said. "I assure you."

"And where will this house arrest be?"

"Here. At the palace."

"Can I ask why?"

"The man fought by my side," said Amoros. "He served our revolution and was heroic. He deserves to be in comfort for his last two days in our country."

Guilt was torturing Amoros, Waters thought, guilt for giving him up to Washington, and after Sewell had left, Waters minced no words in saying so.

"I'm not happy," Amoros said. "That I'll grant."

"It's no consolation."

"I wouldn't think it is. But I meant what I said. You deserve something — good food and rum, a soft bed — before you go."

"How do you know I won't try to kill you?"

Amoros smiled, albeit sadly. "You wouldn't do that."

"Why the hell not?"

"I saved your life. I prolonged it. That's a debt you owe me, and you won't go against that."

"I won't?"

"Jack, my friend, I know you inside and out."

Waters, Isobel, and Amoros had dinner together. At Waters' insistence, it was nothing fancy — roasted chicken with black beans and rice — and they drank from a bottle of honey-brown rum. Other people were in the palace, the building's staff doing their work and Amoros appointees burning the oil in their offices, but everyone gave the three a wide berth so that they could talk. Neither Waters nor Amoros had much to say, and that left Isobel to fill the void. To bring Waters up to date, she described how she'd moved from the embassy residence and bought an unassuming house in town, and how every morning, after coffee and milk, she'd play her piano and get to writing. She was plowing through the pages in her book on Amoros' life and the revolution.

"What's it called?" Amoros asked.

"The Rebellion from the Jungle," Isobel said.

Waters refrained from asking whether she would glorify her subject. Amoros the rebel, when he was leading The Fifty, she could portray as the commander he'd been, fearless, daring, the indefagitable man, but if she showed Amoros in power as a principled human being, the book would transmute into fiction.

"Will I be in it?"

"This is history," Isobel said. "I can't leave your part in the fighting out."

Sleep would not come that night. Waters lay in bed in a second floor room, his clothing, carried over from the jail, around him, and he considered the trust Amoros was feeling to let him spend the night so free. He could walk out the room's door if he chose and try to escape the palace. And if in some way he got past the guards and scaled the fence, though he might not get himself off the island, he could hide out in the bush. He could survive there for weeks. Soldiers on horseback would give pursuit, but he would leave a trail of fire. All he needed were matches and oil, which he could steal from someone's hut, and he could do on this island what William Sherman had done in the South. Amoros and every islander would be made to pay for having interfered with the life of Jack Waters.

He sat up, his heartbeat racing. It would be the defiant thing to do — to go down fighting and take others with him. But he thought, as well, that his musings were lunacy, pride and egoism run amuck, and he looked back on the time in the forest when Amoros had saved his life. On that particular, Amoros was right. If not for Amoros, he would have been dead today. Starkly put, he was in debt to the President even though the President was handing him over for eventual execution. Unless he intended to betray his own precept, that no one should fail to honor a debt, he had to abide by the President's decision to use him as a sacrificial pawn in the political arena. Living up to the ethos he set for himself was what made him better than people like the cheater back home and General Hernandez Garcia Napoles. But should he adhere to his self-imposed code if it hastened death? That seemed insane. Where fate had led him was insane.

Like Amoros and his rebel comrades, he had killed ample numbers of people during the fighting, but this one killing, from a lifetime ago, as just a killing as there could possibly be, would lead to his end. It felt like nothing less than a fiendish joke, cosmic injustice.

Sleepy after his overwrought night, Waters got up when the sun's pink rim edged into his window. His head throbbed and his eyes ached. Though he didn't feel like eating, he asked for coffee. He liked it black and sugary, and a palace attendant brought everything to him, the coffee pot on a salver, brown cubes in his cup. He sat at the table in his room, in no rush to finish the piquant brew, and Amoros came and joined him. In dun-green fatigues, the President meandered around the room, his hair wet from his morning bath, and he told Amoros he had a taxing day ahead, hours of paperwork to do in his office, meetings with the French and Dominican ambassadors.

"You have the run of the palace," he said. "Grounds, too. But the guards will stop you at the fence."

"Can I make a request?"

"Don't say a girl. A girl or a whore. I'm not doing what Garcia did."

"It's not that."

"Tell me then."

"Consider it a dying man's request."

"Say it."

"I want you to kill me yourself," said Waters. "I want to die here, not up in the States like a common criminal."

The idea had germinated overnight, after a dream. If he had to die soon, he would rather have it happen on the island than back in what had been home. Why recognize the United States of America? Why cave to the bastards demanding his extradition? The father of the man he'd stabbed at his house should be sent to him for redress; his seed had helped create that boy. And he wanted to make Amoros execute him because that would bring Amoros pain. He knew the affection Amoros had for him, and he was hoping that if Amoros shot him, the act would stick with the President. Ideally, it would haunt him for life.

"I can't kill you myself," said Amoros. "I couldn't do that."

"What's stopping you?"

"Everything," Amoros said. "We were comrades. You're a hero of the revolution."

"A hero you'd send to his death."

"We've discussed that. The Americans —"

"I'm asking you *as* a comrade."

"I'm the president now. I can't shoot people."

"Make me your last kill."

"Absolutely not."

"You know what they'll do in New Orleans? They'll treat me like a dog and hang me from a tree."

Amoros left for his office, his first appointment of the day, but the expletives he spewed before leaving the room, the grimace on his face, said he'd been jolted. He knew what might happen to Waters in New Orleans, how Waters might be treated for his crime. Mixed and light-skinned though he was, the public would view him as black, and the man he'd murdered had been white. Would Amoros ship him away to face that?

Despite the bleakness of his future, Waters went to sleep that afternoon, and he was waking up, wriggling out of a nightmare, when Amoros returned.

In his dream, people *had* been tying him to a tree.

"Will you do it?"

"I should have put you back in the prison to wait."

"Kill me," Waters said. "Do that and it's over. You can cut off my head and send it to the States. Wouldn't that satisfy the Americans?"

"It could. But the best I can do, I've been thinking about it, is to have you shot by firing squad."

"You," Waters said. "It has to be you."

Waters recommended an execution in town. At the central square, against a wall, he would take his place, and Amoros could tell the crowd that he had bartered his soul for money. Passed over for a government job, he'd stolen from the rebels, Amoros could claim. Or he'd sold himself to the landowners to help them plot a government coup. Whatever Amoros accused him of, it could become the official record.

"I'll go down in infamy," Waters said. "I'll be cursed here for years and you can put me as a traitor in the history books."

"That's what you want?"

"Disgrace!" said Waters. "My name will be dirt."

"That's vanity," Amoros said. "Nothing but vanity."

"It's my due."

"Your due?"

"For what I did for the revolution. I deserve to die how I want."

"Gringo's privilege, is that it?"

"No."

"Yes, it is. Your ambassador demands I turn you over if I want to have good relations with Washington. You demand I do something because it's your due."

"It's a condemned man's wish. Simple as that."

Scott Adlerberg

"It's arrogance, Waters, and it drips off you Americans like sweat."

Back bent, leaning forward, Amoros had his gaunt face inches from Waters'. Blood vessels had popped in the President's eyes, streaking them red, and his teeth, behind his rose-pink lips, were bared. Waters, stepping back, felt himself quivering; a weird supposition filtered through his mind that Amoros would bite or kiss him, in rage over his request or to bid him farewell from life. But Amoros did neither, instead closing his eyes and taking a breath, and when Waters asked him whether he would fulfill his wish for an execution, Amoros said, "Come with me."

A walk began, a march of sorts, with Amoros guiding Waters. He'd ordered two palace guards to join them, and these men, in their green uniforms, flanked Waters. They held rifles. Their boots made clicks on the marble flooring. In their improvised formation, the four of them ascended a flight of stairs, and they proceeded down a hall and through a door to the President's bedroom. Amoros took a holstered pistol off his dresser and attached the holster to his belt. Then they headed back down the corridor and descended the steps to the ground floor. At the palace's entrance, another guard let them through,

234

and they crossed the palace courtyard. They went out the gate to the road. Night was close, the sky purplish, and Amoros continued to lead, with Waters behind and the two guards last. Whoever was out and saw them stopped, though none of the bystanders spoke, and Waters could assume but one thing, that Amoros was taking him to the central square for his execution. *I'll die as I want*, he thought, repressing a smile, and his certitude is why he was not at all ready for what happened to him next.

From out of nowhere came a man on horseback, galloping along the street, a scarf or bandana cloaking his face. The man was carrying a revolver and aimed to fire at Amoros. A hand pushed Waters from behind, a shot or two crackled, and the rider, who never stopped, sped around a house and down another street, gone. Waters fell backwards, bleeding from his chest, and a pinprick of pain blew up into a fire inside him. He felt tears coming; his vision blurred. And he could hear someone talking to him, Amoros, telling him he'd not be forgotten.

"That's a hero's act. You saved my life."

"I—"

"People saw it."

"I did no such thing."

"Gentlemen?"

Amoros was asking the guards.

"Yes, sir. He jumped when the assassin came."

"To block the bullet?"

"Seems so."

"The American who gave his life for me."

Back against the ground, staring up at the President, Waters felt the fluid in his lungs and the blood pooling in his throat, and he did not think he'd be able to say what he wanted to say.

"It'll be in Isobel's book," said Amoros. "I'll tell her. You're a hero."

The President had crouched over him, hands on his knees, face reflective.

"You'll be a hero in our history books."

"No."

"What'd you say?"

Waters tightened every muscle in his body, held himself still, and pushed from deep inside to speak. The pain was excruciating, brought darkness to his eyes, but he got out the answer he wanted heard.

"'No,' I said. Just 'no.'"

And as the darkness became complete, cutting him off from the world, he found the strength to put into words what he hoped to make clear:

"Fuck being a hero," he said. "Fuck heroes and fuck history."

Acknowledgements

Thanks as always to J David Osborne, who took a look at part of this book and said yeah, do the rest, I want it. Thanks also to Jason Starr who had encouraging words to say about an early section I showed him. Two or three readers whose judgment you trust spurring you on. What more do you need to finish a book?

Scott Adlerberg grew up in the Bronx and a wooded suburb just outside New York City. His first book was the Caribbean-set crime novel *Spiders and Flies* (2012). Next came the noir/fantasy novella *Jungle Horses* (2014) and the psychological thriller *Graveyard Love* (2016). Each summer, he hosts the Word for Word Reel talks film commentary series in Manhattan. He lives in Brooklyn.

Other titles from Broken River Books:

The Least of My Scars by Stephen Graham Jones
Peckerwood by Jedidiah Ayres
Street Raised by Pearce Hansen
The First One You Expect by Adam Cesare
Repo Shark by Cody Goodfellow
The Last Projector by David James Keaton
Long Lost Dog of It by Michael Kazepis
Jungle Horses by Scott Adlerberg
Visions by Troy James Weaver
Will the Sun Ever Come Out Again? by Nate Southard
The Blind Alley by Jake Hinkson
On the Black by Ed Dinger
Scores by Robert Paul Moreira
Death Don't Have No Mercy by William Boyle
Everything Used to Work by Robert Spencer

Zero Saints by Gabino Iglesias
Black Gum by J David Osborne
Graveyard Love by Scott Adlerberg
The Heartbeat Harvest by Mark Jaskowski
Chupacabra Vengeance by David Bowles
Heathenish by Kelby Losack
Gravity by Michael Kazepis
Hard Sentences: Crime Fiction Inspired by Alcatraz
edited by
David James Keaton & Joe Clifford
The Snake Handler by Cody Goodfellow
& J David Osborne
Human Trees by Matthew Revert
Itzá by Rios de la Luz

For more information on Broken River Books,
please visit:
www.brokenriverbooks.com

Follow us on Twitter: @brbjdo
Follow us on Instagram: @brbjdo

www.ingramcontent.com/pod-product-compliance
Lightning Source LLC
Chambersburg PA
CBHW020323200626
46814CB00006BB/2387